FIVE DEADLY SHADOWS

They were ruthless killers and their business was kidnapping and the collection of heavy ransoms. But things promised to change when Rick and Hattie Braddock, the frontier's jauntiest private investigators, were signed on as protection for the great star Ella Cardew. The Five Deadly Shadows had never heard of Rick and Hattie. They planned on seizing their richest prize, and demanding the biggest ransom ever. When they made their move, all hell broke loose . . .

LEONARD MEARES

FIVE DEADLY SHADOWS

Complete and Unabridged

LINFORD
Leicester

First published in Great Britain in 1993 by
Robert Hale Limited
London

First Linford Edition
published 2000
by arrangement with
Robert Hale Limited
London

British Library CIP Data

Meares, Leonard F.
  Five Deadly Shadows.—Large print ed.—
Linford western library
  1. Western stories
  2. Large type books
  I. Title
  823.9'14 [F]

ISBN 0–7089–5693–9

Published by
F. A. Thorpe (Publishing)
Anstey, Leicestershire

Set by Words & Graphics Ltd.
Anstey, Leicestershire
Printed and bound in Great Britain by
T. J. International Ltd., Padstow, Cornwall

This book is printed on acid-free paper

1

The Dirtiest Game of All

People watched from the sidewalks the search party's return to Millsville, seat of Porter County, Utah Territory. In charge of the five-man party, the lean, grim-faced Deputy Sheriff Clem Eisley led the horse carrying the slicker-wrapped body. Another of the five, one of the county's physicians, was Jonas Kennedy.

It was Kennedy who growled an answer to the townsfolks' questions.

'Yes, Luke Dixon's son. Dead two days, his throat cut.' Anticipating another question, he added. 'The family knows by now. From Ball Rock Bend, Deputy Eisley sent Marv Hayes west to the Dixon ranch.'

The body of the murder victim was taken to the undertaker's parlour, after

1

which the deputy dispersed the party and hurried to his boss's office. There, the county jailer told him Sheriff Moss Purdy was visiting the office of the local newspaper, the *County Observer*. Minutes later, Eisley was joining his gaunt, bewhiskered boss and editor George Thayer, a veteran of the Fourth Estate, slight of physique and sensitive-featured.

'I'm guessing — from the look on your face . . . ' Purdy began as the deputy helped himself to a chair.

'Yeah,' scowled Eisley. 'Up north near the county line, young Roddy. They just cut his throat and dumped him there. Left no tracks, but you've probably guessed that too.'

'Damn!' breathed Purdy.

Thayer sighed heavily and began filling his pipe.

'Just seventeen years old,' he muttered. 'A good boy and his father's pride and joy. You thinking what I'm thinking, Moss? The ransom note was found by L-Bar-D hands fixed to a line fence. And maybe Luke Dixon should've obeyed the kidnappers' demands. He could afford the thirty thousand. He's the wealthiest cattleman in the territory.'

'And the boy'd be alive now?' challenged Purdy. 'We can't be sure of that, George. Is their word worth anything, the kind of scum who'll grab a hostage?'

'I like Luke Dixon, but he's a powerful man and stubborn,' said Thayer. 'Just can't believe any man anywhere would dare defy him. Power and wealth have gone to his head. So he did exactly what the note warned him against, organized his whole bunkhouse gang to start a search, sent word to you. Then you deputized posses and . . . ' He grimaced. 'All that action signed young Roddy's death warrant. That's what it gets down to.'

'That's *just* what it gets down to,' declared Eisley. He produced a crumpled sheet of paper and passed it to his boss. 'I found that pinned to Roddy's shirt.'

' 'Dixon,' ' Purdy read aloud. ' 'You were warned we mean business.' Damn, butchering bastards!'

'What kind of outlaw trash works such a lousy game?' Eisley moodily wondered.

'Kidnapping,' scowled Purdy. 'The dirtiest game of all.'

'You know . . . ' Thayer lit his pipe and waxed pensive. 'It could happen again. I'm suddenly remembering similar cases. Same routine — so why not the same gang?'

'What're you getting at?' demanded Purdy.

The editor quit his desk and moved to a shelf stacked with back issues of newspapers from other regions. He fossicked a while before locating what he sought, two special editions, one a Wyoming paper, the other from Nevada. Returning to his desk, he blew dust from them and scanned the front page reports.

'Yes, two other such incidents. Well, two we know of. There could've been others.'

'Keep talking,' urged Purdy. 'You don't have to read it all to me. Just give me the gist.'

Thayer summarized the two stories with the sheriff and his deputy hanging on his every word.

The incident reported in the Wyoming paper had occurred a little more than a year ago. Another rancher, obviously not as wealthy as Luke Dixon, had received a demand for $20,000 after his wife's disappearance. She was returning alone by buggy from the local township and, when she was overdue, the rancher and his foreman checked the trail linking his spread to the township and found the empty vehicle, its horse still in harness, a note fixed to the seat.

'That rancher did as they demanded, near bankrupted himself to come up with the money,' said Thayer. 'He left it at the isolated spot nominated, never advised the law authorities, just returned to his ranch as directed.'

'And?' prodded Eisley.

'His wife came home next day, had to walk all the way,' said Thayer. 'She was exhausted, but unharmed, and could offer no description of her abductors. Five of them, hooded and wearing dusters or slickers, no brands on their horses. After seizing her, they kept her blindfolded. Any time she heard them talking, they were too far away for her to hear what they were saying — or even memorize their mode of speech.'

'So no descriptions, no nothing,' mused Purdy. 'And what happened in Nevada?'

The Nevada incident matched the Porter County outrage; it occurred two months later. A banker's daughter was kidnapped. Upon finding the ransom note, he panicked and demanded immediate action by the local law. A full-scale search was mounted and the girl was eventually found — lynched.

A hand-printed note attached to her clothing reminded the banker he had been warned against appealing to the sheriff of that county.

Thayer's hunch shocked Purdy to the core and started the deputy cursing bitterly. The same five unknowns *could* have committed all three crimes. They were anonymous and marauding a wide area and they were deadly efficient and ruthless, slaying their hostages as a warning so that, eventually, no kin of a victim would dare disobey their orders.

'That's the hell of it, Moss,' complained Thayer. 'Wide-spread publicity *after* the event. Their savagery becomes public knowledge while they, the perpetrators, remain safely anonymous. Nobody knows where to look for them nor who to look for. It's a damnable game they're playing — and could make them richer than the people they prey upon.'

'In all my years as a lawman . . . ' Purdy was seething.

7

'They have to be stopped!' raged Eisley.

'Well, damn it, of course they have to be stopped.' Thayer agreed. 'But how can the law nail five unknowns, mere shadows? Newspapers have no option but to circulate such news. When you stop to think about it, it's an obligation, because people should be warned these sons of bitches'll hold to their threats. If it's the same gang, and I'm convinced it is, they've twice proved they'll kill without hesitation.'

'Great Lord Almighty,' mumbled Purdy. 'They could — keep on getting away with it.'

'Satanic cunning, I call it,' declared Thayer. 'At least one of them, maybe all five of them, must be a brilliant tactician.'

'With no conscience,' Purdy said through clenched teeth.

'Totally devoid of conscience, utterly merciless,' said the newspaperman.

★ ★ ★

Some weeks later, in Denver, Colorado, Hattie Braddock returned from a shopping spree. The home and office of this beautiful half of the Braddock Detective Agency was the apartment above the Quinn Brothers barber shop on Aurora Street, accessible by way of a flight of steps on the building's right side. So crossing the street, making for those stairs, she was visible to the brothers, the clients in their chairs and those waiting for haircuts.

'The Belle of Colorado, boys!' she heard the elder brother announce.

The announcement was followed by a gleeful whoop and a whistle or two. These indications of admiration of her good looks could never faze a young woman of Hattie's calibre. She rewarded the gawking men with a bedazzling smile and a cheery wave before climbing the stairs. Men will be men. Why *wouldn't* they ogle the beautiful, blue-eyed blonde with the eye-catching figure that owed nothing to whalebone corsetting?

Letting herself into the parlour that did triple service as office and dining room, she moved to the bedroom to unwrap and admire her purchase, a new gown to complement her complexion and anatomy.

'Where are you at this moment, Rickard James Braddock?' she wondered aloud. 'No doubt sitting behind a pat hand in some well-patronized gambling house. Do your best, darling, and who's complaining? You're a steady winner. By the time you come home for supper, we'll probably be a couple of hundred dollars richer.'

In this era, the term Women's Liberation had never been heard, but Hattie Braddock of the 1880s could justly be considered emancipated, could claim to enjoy the best of both worlds — marriage and career. Rick was no bachelor when the Braddock Detective Agency's poster was first exhibited in the barber shop's street window; they had both established the business. She was more, much more, than the devoted wife of handsome Rick. She was his efficient secretary and, most important of all, his even more efficient partner. When Rick Braddock worked as assigned, Hattie went along, and not just for the ride.

Such was her background, Rick couldn't have found a more reliable co-worker. Orphaned in her teens, she had made her own way before meeting and marrying him. She had been a nursemaid, seamstress and waitress, had tired of those mundane pursuits and involved herself in what could be termed frontier show business, working theatres and travelling tent shows, becoming a better than average actress. As an ingenue she was effective, but wasted. Like her husband, she was a natural in character roles, able to portray women of middle and advanced age with consummate ease; all it took was make-up, the right costume and an instinct for living the role.

As his wife had assumed, Rick Braddock had spent the earlier part of this afternoon at one of Denver's most popular gambling houses. When the poker party broke up, he was ahead, if not by $200. But $160 was a useful boost to their joint bankroll so, when he made his way to a less salubrious establishment, he was in good humour.

The less salubrious establishment was Riley's Bar on Kempner Street. Here, the decor and clientele were a tad rough around the edges, but Riley served cold beer; the beer was to the young private detective's taste and he enjoyed the atmosphere of the place.

Other patrons sparing a glance for the dark-haired, handsome six-footer might have assumed him to be a successful businessman, but would never have guessed him to be an investigator of above-average ability and of a background as chequered as that of his wife. Rick had done it all.

In his youth, he had learned much from a bunko man of genteel demeanour and congenial disposition, a likeable rogue well qualified to tutor an eager-to-learn boy in tricks of his tricky trade. Rick had gone on to try his hand at prospecting and ranch work, but just for starters. He had taught himself to play several musical instruments, had become a wily gambler and was fluent in Spanish and had a smattering of various other languages.

Then he too had joined tent shows and repertory groups plying the frontier. Trick shooting had come easily to him as had all the Thespian arts; he had a flair for characterization and shared Hattie's skill with makeup, for changing his appearance and mode of speech at short notice.

He had half-finished a cool beer and was idly studying the other drinkers when his gaze fell on a portly, dapper little man in a condition of advanced indignation. His garb was of good quality, Rick observed, if a little on the flashy side. Red-faced, he was denouncing the hefty hardcase hovering over him, and loudly.

'You tried to lift my wallet! What kind of a place is this? A man can't enjoy a drink without some pickpocket . . . '

'You callin' me a thief?' challenged the hardcase.

Two other men protested the accusation, declaring the accused was a good friend of theirs and, for good measure, began pushing the little man around. Rick shook his head in a sad, knowing way. Oldest trick in the book, he was thinking. Three lowdowns working together. If the thief were caught in the act, his backups would offer support. The mark would take a beating and would still lose his wallet. As he set his tankard on the bar and began advancing on the group — none of Riley's other customers paid any attention to the disturbance — he was reflecting that Denver's two-bit thieves needed to brush up their act.

'That's all, boys,' he drawled as he arrived. 'Nice try, but it didn't work.' Of the chubby little man he enquired,

'You still have your wallet?'

'Yeah, I'm a big disappointment to this galoot. Shelley's the name, and I appreciate your interest, son.'

'Best leave it at that,' Rick suggested to the truculent trio.

But some never learn. The pick-pocket indicated his disapproval of Rick's intervention by bunching a fist and aiming a blow to his face. Rick dodged, let the fist flash over his left shoulder and retaliated with a hard uppercut. The pick-pocket reeled a few yards to collide with two of Riley's patrons, one of whom suffered the indignity of having his shot of rye knocked out of his hand. He didn't take kindly to that, promptly belly-punched the pickpocket, who gasped a curse and backhanded him.

The first of the pickpocket's accomplices aimed a kick to Rick's groin, but Rick's hands moved faster than that swinging boot. He captured it, then the whole leg, and heaved with all his might. The man yelled, hurtled backwards and crashed against an occupied table. When the occupants thereof began clobbering him, the third backup dashed to his aid.

Portly Mr Shelley was confused by the chain reaction, the bewildering alacrity with which a full-scale brawl erupted. All three would-be thieves were now trading blows with other patrons, chairs were overturning and a spittoon air-borne. Fire-haired Riley was vaulting the bar; not to Rick's surprise, he wielded a shillelagh.

Rick ducked a hurled chair, grasped his arm and said,

'Drop, friend. On your knees.'

'What're we gonna do — *pray*?'

'This is called a tactical retreat,' explained Rick, now on all fours. 'There's a back way out of here. Let's go.'

The little man followed his example. As they crawled through the melee to the rear exit, the ruckus was increasing in intensity, Riley's regulars getting into the spirit of the occasion.

They made it to the back door. Rick raised a hand to grasp and turn the knob and then they were out of there and upright, leaving the mayhem behind them. As they moved along the alley, they dusted themselves off. Shelley was a stranger in town and still shaken by the experience.

'Ordered a drink, didn't get to even sip it before that big jasper jostled me and tried to lift my wallet,' he complained. 'I was just taking a stroll, needing to ponder my problems over a quiet shot of bourbon . . . '

'I didn't finish my drink, come to think of it,' said Rick. 'Well, I know a quieter place not far from here. The Bowman Club. No brawling allowed on the premises. You'll be my guest, Mister Shelley.'

'That's nice, real hospitable. Call me Max. My card.'

By way of a side alley, they reached and crossed Kempner Street. While escorting the little man to the Bowman Club, Rick studied his calling card.

'Max Shelley, Entrepreneur,' he noted. 'I'm impressed — even more impressed that you are agent and manager to the famous Ella Cardew.'

'The toast of 'Frisco,' nodded Max. 'The nightingale of the west coast.'

'I knew she was playing a season here, of course. Posters all over town.'

'Final performance tonight, the Paradise Pavilion. Say, what do I call you, son?'

'Allow me, Max. My card.'

They had almost reached their destination. Max took the card and read aloud,

'Rickard J. Braddock, Braddock Detective Agency. Discretion Guaranteed. So — uh — you're a private dick.'

'It's a living, Max.'

'How's business?'

'Brisk. Why do you ask?'

'I'm getting an idea. Never needed help so badly, Rick. I mean specialized reliable help.'

The agent-manager of the singer as

well known as Lillian Russell herself poured out his tale of woe when they were drinking at a corner table for two in a bar catering to a better class citizen. He made his pitch and won Rick's undivided attention.

Max's star was certainly popular. So far, this tour was a big success, with record ticket sales. From Denver, the company would travel southwest with the expectation of capacity audiences in halls and theatres all the way to Calvo Junction. From there, they would play South Utah, South Nevada *en route* home to San Francisco.

'San Francisco.' Max downed a mouthful and heaved a sigh. 'My hometown — where I wish I was right now. If Ella's a hit, I can book her into the best theatres in 'Frisco, Sacramento, Los Angeles, all the big towns. But, if this tour's a failure, it's back to the chorus line for her. She'll be finished and I'll lose the most popular client I ever handled. I got to tell you, Rick, I need you — I'm desperate. Look, private dicks work as bodyguards, don't they? Just like the Pinkertons?'

'Max, if you're thinking of retaining my services, I'd better explain I can't undertake an assignment without greater knowledge of what's expected of me,' warned Rick. 'You'll have to be more specific.'

'Got to know everything?'

'Anything you confide will be our secret. Now what's the problem? Miss Cardew needs protection from smitten, over-stimulated admirers, stage door mashers? I can handle them, easily.'

'How I wish it was that simple.'

'It's not that simple?'

'Rick, she draws admirers like honey draws flies, but what she needs most is protection from herself.'

The famous singer, Rick learned, was temperamental, imperious, unpredictable and, since the beginning of this tour, had become a compulsive drinker. Drunk or sober, she had the temper of a wildcat. The troupe consisted of five people. Billy Beale, described by Max as the best advance man in the business, always travelled ahead, handled bookings and publicity. Geraldo Palestrina, Ella's accompanist, was a Jack-of-all-trades, helped with the loading of baggage and was a self-taught piano tuner equipped with the right tools; give him an hour and, by the time the curtain went up, the most battered upright would be as finely tuned as a brand-new Steinway.

'And me, I introduce Ella, give the paying customers a big thrill by bragging of the treat in store for them.'

'That makes four of you,' said Rick. 'Who's the fifth party?'

'Haven't you guessed? A big timer like Ella rates a dresser doubling as her maid. But Molly McGovern quits after tonight's show, couldn't take any more. It's a constant battle, Rick, all of us trying to keep Ella sober, heading off locals, hotel clerks and waiters smuggling booze to her. That's how Ella's been getting the stuff. Any backstage sport wanting to visit the great lady, she doesn't want a bouquet or a box of candy. He'd better bring a bottle along.'

'Her dresser can't take any more?'

'Ella gave her a black eye. Molly's been mighty patient, but a girl can only take so much. Believe me, my star is hard on dressers. Since this tour began, Molly's the third dresser who's quit. And the hell of it is she was more experienced than the other two.'

Rick's mind was turning over fast. He finished his beer and eyed Max thoughtfully.

'You really are in a spot,' he remarked. 'I agree your thirsty thrush needs a bodyguard. If my terms are acceptable, I'm your man. But you don't need just me, Max.'

'I've tried,' Max glumly assured him. 'Ella'll raise hell if I can't hire a replacement for Molly, but how am I gonna find a new dresser on such short notice?'

'Fortunately, I can help you there.'

'You know somebody?'

'Just the girl for the job, Max. She's had a lot of experience in theatre work.'

'Who is she?'

'The name's Inger Schmidt.' Rick pulled that one out of thin air. 'Nice kid, eager to please. But tough when she has to be.'

'A kraut girl?'

'Austrian.'

'Can you get her?' demanded Max.

'I know where to find her,' said Rick. 'I also know she's between jobs at this time. Now, before we go any further, let's talk money. I don't come cheap, but that shouldn't bother you. While your star is sober enough to entertain the paying customers, you're a million miles from bankruptcy.'

'Okay, how much?' asked Max.

'For my services, thirty-five dollars a day.'

'That's plus expenses, accommodation — the lot. No argument, Rick. We got a deal. And the dresser?'

'Twenty a day.'

'Hell, Rick, that's a sawbuck more than I was paying Molly.'

'There'll be times when I can't stand guard on Ella,' Rick pointed out. 'I can't be there when she's dressing or in her bedroom or taking a bath. For twenty and found, you get Inger, and she'll be more than maid and dresser. She'll watch your star when I can't.'

'For fifty-five bucks a day . . . ' began Max.

'You get a male bodyguard, a maid, a dresser *and* a female bodyguard,' declared Rick. 'That's what it adds up to. That's what you need. And Inger won't quit on you, nor will your star break her spirit as she broke Molly's. So?'

'Deal,' nodded Max. 'Listen, you sure this Schmidt girl can take care of herself? You closely acquainted with her?'

'I've known her quite a time,' said Rick. 'She trusts me, Max, and she won't let you down. I'll go talk to her right-away.'

'It'll mean you'll both have to pack your grips and be at the railroad depot by eight o'clock tomorrow morning,' said Max. 'That's if I decide this kraut dame can cut the mustard. Can you fetch her to the Paradise Pavilion for the last show?' He delved into a pocket and offered two tickets. 'Fourth row front. Bring her backstage after the show so I can look her over and introduce you. You'll hit it off with Geraldo. *He's* not temperamental. But Ella?' He shrugged helplessly. 'Get ready to duck.'

'We'll be there,' Rick promised.

Soon afterward, he was rejoining his wife. She greeted him affectionately.

'Mississippi Rick, the gambling dandy in person. For richer, for poorer, we said when we exchanged vows. So what's the good word, darling? Are we richer or poorer?'

'A hundred and sixty in front,' he told her. 'And we'll be doing better. I picked up another assignment for us. Honey, you're gonna love this one.' He moved to the kitchen entrance and sniffed appreciatively. 'Smells great. Can we dine any earlier?'

'I can hustle supper along,' she nodded. 'Stay with me. I want to hear about the assignment.'

In the kitchen and later during their early supper, he dealt it all out for her in detail. And much to her delight.

'Dresser to the great Ella Cardew!' she enthused. 'Think of it, Rick. On the road again. Back in show business. Not performing, but who cares? The lights, the action backstage, the smell of greasepaint . . . '

'And the great star's a wildcat with a thirst that won't quit,' he reminded her. 'It won't all be fun. A drunk, male or female, can be hard to handle and so damn devious.'

'For her sake, I can be patient and watchful,' she murmured. 'I'm sorry for her already. With her looks and talent, that beautiful voice, it's tragic she should suddenly become a hard drinker.'

'Suddenly?'

'That's what I said. I've read every newspaper and magazine story ever published about her. Well, most of them. Never a hint she's overly fond of liquor. So it must be a recent problem.'

'You're probably right, sweetheart. Interesting notion. If either of us found out why she's hitting the bottle, we might help her overcome her problem. That's not what Max is paying us for, but it'd be quite an achievement, wouldn't it?'

'My loveable Rick.' She smiled fondly. 'Tall, tough and handsome — *very* tough when needs be, ruthless even — but soft hearted too.'

'We're in for a busy night,' he warned. 'Have to pack before and after the show, get a good night's sleep and make the depot before eight tomorrow morning. Well, we'll be on time. For this job, I don't need a

27

disguise, and you don't need to ring many changes.'

'Too bad I can't wear my new gown to the theatre,' she shrugged. 'On humble Inger Schmidt it would be out of character. Never mind. I'll look the part.'

'With your colouring, it'll be easy,' he suggested.

'Nothing to it,' she chuckled. 'With my hair plaited in the style of a typical Rhine maiden, I'll pass.'

'Much as we admire Max's beautiful star, we'd better be ready for anything,' Rick cautioned her. 'You, honey, have to be extra careful. Don't forget the dresser you're replacing is wearing a shiner.'

'If Ornery Ella wants to play rough, I'll protect myself in my own way,' shrugged Hattie. 'Max Shelley needn't worry. She won't cause adverse comment by appearing on stage with a black eye or a red nose, but she could be wearing a bruise or two where they don't show.'

★ ★ ★

While the Braddocks dined early this day, while sundown was still ninety minutes away, a man named Noah Gannon began his slow crossing of an expanse of flats a hundred and fifty miles from Denver and some ten miles west of the northern reaches of the Sawatch Mountains. In age, he was just on the south side of forty. He was blond and blunt-featured, straddling a black gelding with white socks. A satchel was secured to his saddle. He was unarmed.

Gannon was the latest victim of the five deadly unknowns recently discussed in the office of a Utah newspaper. To meet their demands, he had been obliged to beg a loan from a bank at Deansburg, his hometown.

Steadily, he approached the copse dead ahead, the only vegetation on the flats. He estimated the distance, having memorized every detail of the ransom demand, and reined up twenty yards from the trees. Almost immediately, a man showed himself. His hood was held in place by his flat-brimmed hat. He wore a duster, making it impossible for Gannon to speculate as to his physique. He looked to be six feet tall, but could have been burly or lean; no way of guessing. In his right hand, he hefted a cocked six-gun. His left hand was clamped to the shoulder of a frightened seven-year-old boy, Gannon's son.

Nothing was said. The man gestured for Gannon to move closer. Gannon nudged his mount forward another six yards, then obeyed another pantomimed command and reined up again. With his pistol, the man pointed to the satchel. Gannon detached and tossed it. It fell at the man's feet. He removed his left hand from the boy's shoulder long enough to pick it up and toss it over his shoulder into the trees. Gannon didn't hear it drop; somebody had been waiting to catch it.

With the man again gripping his

shoulder, the boy matched stares with his father. Gannon spoke gently.

'Toby, you all right?'

'Yes, Pa.'

Gannon clung tightly to his nerves and waited it out. The money was being counted, he reflected. Well, naturally. A few more minutes and his ears caught the sound from within the copse; a man had snapped his fingers. Toby Gannon's guard removed his hand and gestured. The boy hurried to his father, who leaned down with hand extended. In a moment, he was astride, perched behind Gannon, arms wrapped about him.

A gesture of dismissal and Gannon wheeled the black and began recrossing the flats. He glanced back only once. The hooded man was still there, armed with a rifle now and following his retreat through binoculars. Gannon rode on.

'They hurt you?' he demanded.

'Only once, Pa. When I was scared — crying — one of 'em slapped me.'

'They do anything else to you?'

'No, Pa.'

'They feed you?'

'Some. Not much. I'm real hungry.'

'You won't be for long. Soon as we get home, you'll have a hot bath and then your Aunt Ruby'll be dishing up something good for you, her fine beef stew, big wedge of apple pie. You'll sleep safe tonight and you and me'll talk when you wake up.'

'I can talk now, Pa. I'm hungry, but I can talk.'

'Good boy. How many of 'em?'

Toby could tell his father precious little about the kidnappers. Five of them. Masked all the time. He had never heard their voices. Maybe they did their talking when he was asleep.

Noah Gannon had been careful, had glimpsed rather than stared at the hand gripping his son's shoulder. If the hooded man had become even vaguely suspicious, he was in no doubt he'd be a dead widower now and his son dead beside him. It would take only two bullets from that Colt.

'Ever notice that man's hand, the one who brought you out to the timber?' he asked. 'It was on your shoulder. I thought I saw — some kind of blue mark.'

'Sure, Pa. He's the one slapped me. I remember.'

'Looked like a tattoo.'

'What's a . . . ?'

'Never mind, Toby. We'll talk some more later. Let's get home.'

Noah Gannon, ex-ranch-hand, now a storekeeper, had made a decision.

Mentally, he was swearing an oath of vengeance.

2

'She's Got Everything'

The return of the kidnap victim and his father to Deansburg was low key. Few citizens had paid any attention when Gannon rode out; it was nearing sundown when he rode in, and he approached the store he ran in partnership with his brother-in-law by way of the back alley. As seen from the street, it was a double-storied building identified by its shingle as the GANNON & EDWARDS GENERAL EMPORIUM.

When they entered the kitchen from the rear, the boy was at once embraced by his aunt. The slender Ruby Gannon Edwards tight-reined her emotions and insisted Toby be fed at once; his bath could wait. Her husband, Dave Edwards, traded solemn nods with Gannon.

'It went off like they wanted,' he guessed.

'Just like they set it up,' muttered Gannon. 'We got Toby back — and they're ten thousand dollars richer.'

His brother-in-law, a lean, sensitive-featured man with a tendency to stoop-shoulderedness, remarked business was quiet at this hour; he might as well close up for the day.

The two men refrained from discussion until the early supper was over and Ruby upstairs with her nephew. Despite contrasting backgrounds, they had become friends and confidants. Until his sister's marriage, Gannon had been a ranch-hand, one of the steady kind, a moderate drinker, a non-gambler saving as much as possible of his earnings. Edwards, a typical townman, had always believed he had a future in merchandising. He too had been a saver. After Ruby became his wife, Gannon had agreed they should pool their savings to set themselves up in business.

It had been no great wrench for Gannon, abandoning the life of a working cowhand. His own marriage had been tragically short, his wife dying after bearing his son. So, to young Toby, Ruby was a combination of aunt, big sister and mother figure.

'You know how Ruby and I feel about the boy,' Edwards said softly. 'It was as much our decision as yours, Noah. No chances taken. The ransom *had* to be paid.'

'Getting him back unharmed was all that mattered,' agreed Gannon. 'You don't have to be able to read my mind. You can guess how thankful I feel right now. But now I'm worried, and you and Ruby have to be worried. Getting ten thousand together took all our ready cash plus a loan from the bank, a loan it'll take us years to pay off.'

'We're running this store at a steady profit,' shrugged Edwards.

'Dave, it's a loss we can't afford. Toby means everything to me. He's a good kid and — he's my memory of Kate. But I'll be damned if I'm gonna leave it at that. The scum who grabbed Toby, they've probably done it all before — and gotten away with it. Hell, Dave, *somebody's* got to do something!'

'The law . . . '

'How can the law help? We followed orders, kept the whole lousy deal a secret. I didn't dare turn to Marshal Dowd for help. But Toby's safe now, back where he belongs, and you and Ruby'll look out for him. I don't know how long it'll take, but . . . '

'For pity's sake, Noah. How long *what* will take?'

'I said somebody has to do something. Might be I'm that somebody.'

'You? Going alone? Trying to track down five cunning bad-men. No, the risks're too great. They'd ambush you — even if you could find track of them.'

'Don't get me wrong, Dave. I'm not dreaming up rash notions. And I'm gonna be mighty careful. Won't be the first time I've bird-dogged hostiles. I was helping to run down rustlers long before I met Kate, way back when I was a lot younger. Not just rustlers. Redskins. I'll be fine. I've been a storekeeper seven years, but I've forgotten nothing I learned in the old days.'

'You're careful? *Kidnappers're* careful. How can you hope to . . . ?'

'I think I got a chance — an edge. Other fathers've paid their price. You could make book on that. They're pros. But maybe I got something the other victims never had.'

'An edge?'

'That's what I said,' nodded Gannon. His sister rejoined them to announce she had tucked Toby into bed; he was waiting to say goodnight to his father. 'That's fine.' Gannon rose from his chair. 'Uh — I'm trying to remember. Decks of cards. Whereabouts in the store?'

'The shelf left of the counter,'

frowned Ruby. 'With the stationery.'

Before leaving the kitchen, he told his brother-in-law.

'It's okay to let her in on it. Then I won't have to do as much talking to her. But it's our secret, savvy?'

A few moments later he was squatting on the edge of his son's bed, slipping the cards from their thin cardboard container. Toby managed a grin and assured him he felt fine now, but sleepy. Then,

'You don't play cards, Pa.'

'Nope, never have, son. But, before you hit the hay, I want you to think of something again.'

'Sure. What?'

'That mark on the back of the man's hand. You were closer than I was and you'd noticed it before. Remember the shape?'

'Well — maybe.'

Gannon spread the cards, picked up the ace of diamonds and showed it to him.

'Not a diamond, huh?' The boy

shook his head. 'No. Didn't look like a diamond to me. How about this?'

He showed the ace of hearts. Toby squinted at it.

'Kind of like that, Pa. But not exactly.'

'That's what I thought,' nodded Gannon. 'More like this?'

His pulse quickened. Toby was identifying the ace of spades, no hesitation.

'That's it, Pa. Like a heart, but with that little bit pokin' out . . .'

'And it was blue,' Gannon thoughtfully recalled. 'A blue spade tattoo.'

'What's a . . . ?'

'Don't worry about it. And, listen, don't worry about me while I'm gone. I mean, even if I'm gone quite a while.'

'You goin' away?'

'It's just business. Your Aunt Ruby and Uncle Dave'll take care of you, and you be good for 'em, hear?'

'Sure, Pa.'

Gannon repackaged the deck, rose,

drew up the covers and turned the lamp low. For a long moment, he smoothed his son's hair. With his eyes closed and sleep claiming him, the boy's facial resemblance to his dead mother was striking. He quit the room quietly, descended to the store, replaced the deck of cards and moved into the kitchen again to find Dave sitting quiet and Ruby filling a gunnysack.

'Just a few provisions,' she said bitterly. 'Enough to keep you eating until you can shoot fresh meat. If you *must* play man-hunter . . . '

'Sis, don't get mad,' he frowned. 'And listen, both of you. It's important you savvy why I'm doing this.'

'You don't have to explain,' she said. 'I know what you're thinking.'

In a vain attempt to ease the tension, he grinned at his brother-in-law and remarked.

'All women're mind readers, always claiming they know what we're thinking — you ever notice?'

41

'Five dangerous men dared to steal your son, so you have to play lone avenger,' she accused. 'You'll take your rifle along, buckle on your six-shooter for the first time in years and — you've convinced yourself you can find and punish them all.'

'Hey, you're my sister, you're supposed to know me pretty good, so you oughtn't believe what you just said,' he gently chided. 'Now I'm telling you both, and I only want to have to say this the one time, because I ought to get some sleep. I want to make an early start tomorrow, plan on riding out before sun-up.'

'All right, Noah,' said Dave. 'We're listening.'

'I hate those two-legged wolves more than I've hated anybody in my whole life,' declared Gannon. 'But that's not why I have to try finding 'em. What they did to Toby and me, they've likely done to others, and they'll keep on doing it till they're stopped. I don't fool myself I can stop 'em all by myself, but I know I can help. I've got just one thing going for me, a little thing. Even so, it's a lead, a clue that could help identify one of 'em. When I find that one man, I'll parley with the law. If we can identify one of 'em, we can maybe round up all of 'em. That's what I aim to do, so better you wish me luck than try to talk me out of it. I'm doing this for the four of us, and the store. You see, when those lowdowns're rounded up, there's a fair chance we'll get our money back.'

They eyed him intently.

'Well,' sighed Ruby. 'If you give me your word you'll take no foolish risks, not try to be a hero . . . '

'Count on it,' he said.

'One little thing,' frowned Dave. 'And it's a clue?'

'It's something to start with,' nodded Gannon. 'And telling it to a badge-toter or a newspaper-man'd be a dumb mistake. The Deansburg law'd tip off lawmen all over the territory. And the newspapers? They'd spread the word far

43

and wide. Sooner or late, this kidnap gang'd pick up a newspaper and know I've got that one little clue. That'd warn 'em off. They might decide to quit while they're ahead, split up — and nobody'd ever hear of 'em again.'

'They'd get away with it,' mused Dave. 'All the ransom money they've collected, the killings, all the misery they've caused.'

'Can't let that happen,' declared Gannon. 'I just hope you both understand.'

Mid-morning of the morrow, armed, provisioned and carrying as much cash as he anticipated he would need, he was crossing the flats again, making for the copse where the kidnappers had awaited him. Would he be lucky enough to cut sign of the five?

He could only hope.

★ ★ ★

The Braddocks joined the capacity audience for Ella Cardew's last Denver performance and were settled into their seats when the curtain rose, Rick black-suited and as well-groomed as any male present, Hattie well and truly in character as Inger Schmidt, an Austrian girl of humble origins, good character and Teutonic common sense. Rick considered her costume the perfect disguise; trust Hattie to get it right.

Her gown was no-nonsense checked gingham, her headgear a narrow-brimmed, flat-crowned straw hat with two artificial berries and one felt flower its only adornment. Devoid of make-up, she presented a well-scrubbed, healthy, capable look befitting her new identity.

First to appear on stage to polite applause was Max Shelley, resplendent in white tie and tails and reminding Hattie of a tubby penguin. He was the archetypal master of ceremonies, delivering his spiel to the packed house with great aplomb.

'I like him already,' decided Hattie.

'Sure, you'll get along with Max,' predicted Rick. 'He's our kind of people, honey. And we'd better keep remembering he's got trouble aplenty. Her name's Ella Carew.'

Max was introducing his star's accompanist.

'I present to you, ladies and gentlemen, the distinguished, the brilliant master of the pianoforte, who has performed before all the crowned heads of Europe, the renowned, the illustrious — *Signor* Geraldo Palestrina!'

Also in white tie and tails, a short man of slight physique made his entrance. He sported a mane of glossy black hair and flashed white teeth in a beguiling smile. The audience accorded him a resounding ovation. He bowed low, straightened up and raised his hands in appeal, as though overcome by such adulation.

'What a ham,' giggled Hattie.

'I guess we like him too,' grinned Rick.

The accompanist retreated to the grand piano and stood to attention beside it. Max beamed at the expectant crowd and made his final announcement.

'And now, music lovers of the great city of Denver, it is my honour, my privilege, to introduce again the darling of San Francisco, the beloved nightingale of the west coast, the one and only — Madam Ella Cardew!'

The star emerged from stage right, moving majestically to the footlights, her magnificent figure sheathed in a green satin gown with deep cleavage, gesturing carefully with a fan, a gleaming tiara crowning her lustrous blonde hair. While the crowd was in uproar, Rick leaned closer to his wife and, from the side of his mouth, remarked.

'In colouring, she reminds me of you.'

'She's beautiful,' declared Hattie.

'About your height,' he observed. 'And the same great build.'

'The grand champion of all flatterers,' she smiled.

'It's starting to bore you?'

'*That'll* be the day.'

47

The singer moved to centre stage. With a wave to the crowd, Max retreated to the wings. The accompanist seated himself, sweeping his coattails back. He sounded a chord and the performance began and, when Ella Cardew's clear soprano caressed their ears, the people lapsed into reverent silence. She began with a popular ballad and, by intermission, had thrilled one and all with part of her extensive repertoire. It included arias from grand opera, more popular ballads and even renditions of folk songs; the audience was hers when the curtain came down, the applause was thunderous.

Rick and Hattie stayed in their seats and traded opinions.

'A well-trained voice, and she uses it well,' Rick commented. 'I'll be seeking the answer to a question when we become her official bodyguards.'

'And I can guess the question,' frowned Hattie. 'Why does she risk it? She has it all, Rick. The voice, the looks, the fame. Temperament I can understand, but a craving for the cup that cheers — and prematurely ages?'

'No wonder Max's nerves are jumping,' said Rick. 'A little of what she likes'll never hurt her. Too much of it and the ravages begin; first the complexion, then the figure and finally the voice, her tonal quality, the perfect pitch, the perfect timing.'

'Some assignment this'll be,' she predicted. 'But, one way or another, the Braddocks'll win out, just like the other times.'

The second half of the programme was even better. By the time she finished her last encore, Ella Cardew had her audience upright and cheering. The ultimate tribute, a standing ovation. Max reappeared beaming. The accompanist, with a fine show of emotion, raised the star's hand to his lips and bowed low over it; he also clicked his heels.

'Now we go backstage to be introduced,' said Rick, helping his wife from her seat.

'You mean presented, as at court.'

'Did you remember to . . . ?'

'Don't worry. My wedding ring's in my purse.'

'Good girl. Important point, sweetheart. From here on, you're a fraulein, not a frau. Let's go.'

The stagedoor man was big and tough and could not be bribed by heavy-breathing Denver men trying to get past him. When Rick was able to confront him and identify himself and the maiden clinging to his arm, the hefty guardian of the backstage area jerked a thumb.

'Yeah, you're expected. Keep comin'.'

They were met by Max, who ran a critical eye over Hattie.

'Fraulein Schmidt, Max,' offered Rick. 'Take my word, she's just the girl you need — you *and* your big attraction.'

'*Gute Nacht, Herr* Shelley.' Hattie bobbed a curtsy.

'Well . . .' began Max.

'Call her Inger,' urged Rick. 'Just

give the kid a break and I guarantee she won't let you down.'

'You — uh — explained everything?' frowned Max.

'She knows the deal,' Rick assured him.

'I wonder if either of you could guess how rough it's gonna be,' winced Max. 'I'll take you to Ella's dressing room and you'll see for yourselves.'

In the dressing room, they found Ella, in a negligee, snapping abuse at a plump young woman in street clothes; the star had a sharp tongue and her ex-dresser was close to tears. The accompanist appeared almost as nervous. Molly McGovern, her left eye still swollen, complained to Max.

'I can't take any more, Mister Shelley. Thanks for paying me off — and for the bonus — but I'm leaving now.'

'All the luck, kid,' muttered Max, as he ushered her out. 'And thanks for trying.'

After the McGovern girl left, Geraldo

relieved Ella of a glass and a water carafe, took a sniff and rolled his eyes.

'*Momma mia!* Gin!'

He threw glass and carafe out the window, then ducked as the irate Ella swung at him; to Rick's experienced eye, it seemed he'd had a lot of practice.

'You lousy, fake wop!' she screamed.

'Ease up, Ella, for Pete's snake,' begged Max. 'Here's your new dresser. Her name's Inger Schmidt . . . '

'A damn kraut,' sneered Ella.

'*Bitte?*' blinked Hattie.

'Austrian, Miss Cardew,' Rick said smoothly.

'From Blitzenberg, souse of Vienna,' offered Hattie.

'*Prego, signorina*,' Geraldo pleaded in anguish. 'Don'ta say souse arounda here!'

'Well, well, well!' Ella's blue eyes fixed on Rick. 'Who's the handsome dude?'

While Max introduced Rick and

explained his and Hattie's duties, Rick countered the star's intent scrutiny with a polite nod. As well as her beauty, her cunning and her fiery temper, he was conscious of the perfume in this room. It was distinctive. And strong. He made a mental bet it pervaded the entire Paradise Pavilion and at least a block of the street outside.

He knew he was being sized up. Already, he guessed, Ella Cardew was assessing her chances of enslaving him to her beauty. Minus make-up, she was still a knockout and pegging him for a potential provider of hard liquor. Right now, in her eyes, he was a pushover. What a surprise was in store for her!

When Max stopped talking, Ella eyed Hattie coldly and declared.

'You won't last a week. And, while you *are* with us, never call me fraulein, understand? To hired help like you, I'm madam. That clear?'

'*Ja*, Madam.' Hattie bobbed a curtsy. 'I take good care of you. *Sehr gut*.'

'So okay now, you all know the

arrangements.' Max presented Rick with railroad tickets. 'Be at the depot on time in the morning.'

'Count on us,' said Rick. He aimed another nod at Ella before leading Hattie out. 'Miss Cardew, this assignment'll be a pleasant one for me.'

'Time will tell,' drawled Ella.

When the Braddocks had left, Max nodded to Geraldo, who stepped clear of Ella on his way out. She began a bitter complaint while her manager was still closing the dressing room door.

'A kraut for a dresser and private dick, a bodyguard you call him. Max Shelley, you're going too far. I don't have to take this. It's interference with my personal liberties. If I want to enjoy an occasional drink, that's nobody else's business — including yours.'

'If you're finished . . . ' he began.

'Nothing in our contract gives you the right to make a teetotaller of me!' she fumed.

'Damn it, Ella, as your agent and manager, I'm responsible for your welfare both as a person and a performer,' he retorted. 'If you're ever seen drunk on stage, you're finished and so am I. In 'Frisco, Chicago or New York I'll be called the second-rater who couldn't keep you on the wagon.' He resorted to wheedling. 'Proud of your looks, aren't you? Booze could line your gorgeous face and put a lot of weight on that famous figure.'

'Bull,' she sneered. 'My figure's the envy of every woman in show business.'

To emphasize this claim, she sucked in her midriff, causing her well-rounded bosom to heave defiantly. After appraising her generous frontage, he assured her,

'I'm keeping abreast of the weight situation. That's how I know — and *you* know — you'll soon start spreading unless you sign the pledge. Ella, honey, we got a big problem. It wouldn't be a problem at all if you took an occasional snifter and if you knew when to stop, but you *don't* know when to stop. And that's crazy. You don't *have* to be a drunk.'

'I need to drink, need the comfort of it, and I'll tell you why!' she cried. 'I hate being on the road, do you hear? I hate these wild west tours, the one-night stands, the rubes who gawk at me and wouldn't know if I were on or off key, wouldn't know Verdi from Gilbert and Sullivan, wouldn't know if I were singing an aria or 'Oh, Dem Golden Slippers'. The whole thing bores me! I can't stand to be bored and, when I'm bored, I need a drink!'

'Listen . . . ' Max insisted on having the last word. 'We're booked solid and we need this tour. If it's a success, we'll all be a lot richer. If you mess up, the critics'll pan us and we'll be laughed out of the business. Now get dressed and let's head back to the hotel so you can get all the beauty sleep you need.'

★ ★ ★

56

At this time, in the township of Huerta Springs some distance southeast of Denver, five men were in conference in a hotel suite. Barton Renshaw, leader of the group specializing in abduction for profit, was the most ruthless of the five, the most dangerous. He, the planner, the organizer and sometimes executioner, was living proof that appearances can be deceptive.

Seated at a table, checking a map and perusing a recent edition of the Denver *Clarion*, he had the look of a lowly clerical worker, a bookkeeper perhaps, a ribbon clerk in a haberdashery store, a meek and mild reception clerk of a second-rate hotel. He was of slight build and, like his minions, wore town clothes. His suit was of sober colour and design. Brown hair receded from the wide forehead. The face was thin, the features nondescript, the slate-grey eyes devoid of expression. He seemed oblivious to the muttered conversation of his associates. They sensed he was planning another coup and kept their voices low.

The bulky, blond man was Joe Walston. The lantern-jawed rogue with the perpetually sardonic expression was Wes Trent. Seated next to him was the cheerful, moon-faced Waldo Noad. The fifth man was Horrie Langland, a heavyset redhead.

They were a mixed quartet, but had one thing in common with the man whose orders they obeyed without question — contempt for the lives of their victims and for relatives of those victims, the people who mourned them.

Walston, while butting a cigar, glanced briefly at the tattoo on the back of his left hand. Renshaw had always disapproved that tattoo; he was expected to wear gloves, to keep that mark concealed. Right now, he was remembering the switch in Utah, $10,000 delivered by a storekeeper name of Gannon for the safe return of his brat son. Could Gannon — or the kid — have noticed the tattoo? He decided that was unlikely and, at the same time, congratulated himself. Between picking up the money and rejoining his companions, he had thought to don his gloves. Just as well. Bart might have turned mean. And Bart had a temper and a fast right hand. The speed with which Bart could draw that cut-down .32 from his armpit holster was intimidating.

Renshaw cleared his throat fussily. Walston and the others promptly stopped talking. A meticulous man, Renshaw, precise, businesslike, his voice soft but compelling.

'Our next venture, gentlemen, will be most profitable,' he announced. 'Yes, indeed. For such a hostage, I believe I'll insist on one hundred thousand dollars, not a cent less.'

'By Judas,' breathed Langland. 'You're talking big, Bart. Biggest take yet.'

'In comparison, our last take was peanuts,' grinned Noad.

'I did explain, Waldo, that our

business in Utah was intended to serve only one purpose,' Renshaw said testily. 'I settled for a smaller profit from that storekeeper fellow just to keep in practice. That's important, I hope you understand. We succeed through efficiency, and efficiency can only be maintained by practice.'

'Sure, Bart.' Noad had stopped grinning. 'You made that real clear. We all understand.'

'Who's worth a hundred thousand, Bart?' asked Trent.

'This Cardew woman,' said Renshaw, his eyes on the newspaper again. 'Apparently somewhat of a celebrity. A singer from San Francisco currently on tour.'

'Ella Cardew?' frowned Walston. 'Celebrity's the word, Bart. Big name. As famous as Lillie Langtry.'

'Quite so,' nodded Renshaw. 'A most successful tour, according to this paper. Packed houses. Patrons paying a high price for tickets. So I have no doubt this Shelley fellow, her manager, will pay *my* price. Of course I'll allow him time to organize the required sum through his west coast contacts. It's hardly likely he could produce a hundred thousand dollars on short notice.'

Langland chuckled softly.

'You've always said publicity's important to us,' he reminded Renshaw. 'Hell, Bart, *this* job'll be talked about — all over the country — for years to come!'

'After the event, Horace,' countered Renshaw. 'Mister Shelley will be required to abide by the usual terms. The transaction will not become news until the return of the lady, by which time we'll be far from the scene and secure in our anonymity. Like the others, she'll never see our faces nor hear our voices.'

'So there'll be no way she can describe us,' nodded Trent.

'It'll take smart planning, Bart,' remarked Noad. 'But you'll figure it right. You're the expert.'

'Audacity can be most rewarding,'

Renshaw said calmly. 'The unexpected. Lawmen — in particular — are always confused by the unexpected.' He gestured to the paper. 'Most accommodating of the *Clarion*. This coverage of the Cardew tour is extremely comprehensive. The entire itinerary if you please. Names of every town at which she'll perform after the Denver engagement, dates, full particulars, even her retinue. Mode of travel also. Yes, most obliging of the Fourth Estate, always a reliable source of information.'

'Some one-horse burg along their route,' Walston supposed.

'Probably,' said Renshaw. 'And time is on our side, gentlemen. By travelling at night while the company is spending its time in various theatres and hotels, we'll easily stay ahead, checking the possibilities of places at which Miss Cardew is scheduled to appear.'

'Grabbing her on the quiet, getting it done without any hullabaloo, *that'll* be quite a trick,' frowned Langland. 'Big shot showfolks're scarce ever alone.'

'Yeah,' agreed Walston. 'It won't be easy, but Bart's careful planning's our ace in the hole.'

'There are times when the most illustrious of people, the wealthiest, even kings or presidents, can be found unattended,' declared Renshaw. He tapped his temple with a well-manicured finger. 'One only needs to think, to exercise the brain.'

'That's why you're our boss,' grinned Noad. 'Comes to thinking things out, I've never known your equal.'

'Such problems sometimes call for intense mental concentration,' said Renshaw. 'Just as often, however, the answer is quite obvious. In the case of this Cardew woman, for instance, or any other woman, there are occasions upon which they are completely alone. Privacy. You hadn't thought of that? When is she most likely to be alone, nobody watching her?' His cohorts eyed him expectantly. He grimaced and shook his head. 'When sleeping, confound it.'

'Oh, sure,' said Trent, and snapped his fingers.

'When bathing,' Renshaw said impatiently. 'When performing . . . ' He phrased it delicately, 'natural bodily functions.'

'Why didn't I think of that?' chuckled Noad.

'You aren't Bart,' was Langland's prompt rejoinder.

'Not that I'm suggesting we should abduct her from a privy,' shrugged Renshaw. 'But a bedroom or a bathroom, yes, favourable possibilities there.'

'So we're leaving . . . ?' prodded Walston.

'Tomorrow morning,' said Renshaw. 'Early. And, as usual, separately. You'll now return to your hotels.' He consulted his watch. 'We will rendezvous exactly one mile from this town along the south trail at precisely a quarter before eight.' As his men began leaving, he patted the newspaper complacently. 'Most informative, most useful. Everything we need to know.'

3

On Closer Acquaintance

The Braddocks made it to the depot with time to spare and relished the hustle and bustle of the departure of the great star and her increased entourage. Geraldo was an old hand at the hectic routine of supervising loading of their gear into the baggage car, and Max as businesslike as ever.

'Got a wire from Billy,' he informed everybody as they boarded the first Pullman car. 'Our one-night stand at Steeple Rock's a sell-out, gonna be standing room only.'

As was customary when the troupe travelled by railroad, Ella had a private compartment to herself, with Max and Geraldo sharing the next one along. Rick and Hattie were seated nearby, just across the aisle. The train steamed out on schedule and, unbeknown to Ella, she was under Rick's strict surveillance. Already, with Max's authorization, he had visited the baggage car and made a thorough search of her trunk and other baggage for secreted booze. As soon as the southbound was clear of Denver, he entered her compartment, searched it and checked the bag she kept with her.

During this, he was subjected to abuse in somewhat unladylike language, all of which he coolly ignored. Then, when he was about to leave her, she abruptly simmered down and murmured an invitation.

'Sit with me a while. We might as well get acquainted.'

He sat opposite her with his hat on his knees and was intently scrutinized. In her height of fashion travelling outfit, she was beautiful. Also, as he well knew, devious. She led off by enquiring as to his marital status. He replied he was a bachelor, adding,

'Well, theoretically.'

'Ladies man,' she decided.

'Depends on the ladies,' he shrugged.

She offered a ravishing smile which, he felt sure, had quickened many a pulse.

'You know, I'd really appreciate your buying me an occasional drink. Gin, good whisky, a fine cognac, any liquor at all, provided it's high quality. And you'll learn I can be *very* appreciative.'

To her chagrin, he shook his head sadly.

'You don't look like, and you couldn't be, just a drunkard, Ella. You have too much style. It's become a game with you, a contest, right? You have a wayward streak, so you enjoy keeping Max worried by fighting all his efforts to keep you sober.'

'I despise snoopers!' she snapped. 'Especially the kind who think they can read my mind! Get out!'

'You're the star, I'm just your bodyguard,' he acknowledged as he rose to leave. 'But I've got you figured, lady, and I give value for money, always do what I'm paid to do. As long as I'm around, you'd better forget booze. Close surveillance is my speciality.'

He closed the door and moved across the aisle to join Hattie. Quietly, he repeated his brief conversation with the thorn in Max Shelley's side.

'You'll have to stay sharp,' he warned. 'If she doesn't try wheedling you into playing barkeep to her, she may have other tricks up her sleeve.'

'So she made a play for you?'

'Well, she thinks I'm single.'

'If you'd told her you're supporting a wife, five kids and a whole tribe of in-laws, she'd still have tried to seduce you. That's what I'll be remembering if she tries anything on *me* — including rough stuff.'

'Smitty, you're beautiful when you're jealous.'

'*Vielen Dank, liebling.*'

During lunch in the dining car, Ella threw another tantrum. Max, Geraldo and Rick in particular kept close tabs

68

on her and, when the drink steward presented himself, promptly dismissed him.

'Three damn killjoys!' she raged.

'Protectors,' insisted Max. 'Believe me, Ella, there'll come a time you'll thank us.'

'Whata we do, we do for you, *bello signorina*,' Geraldo earnestly assured her.

Hattie was seated in another part of the car, enjoying her lunch until, under the table, she felt a hand on her knee. The thin-moustached dude seated opposite her had been appraising her lecherously and voicing a suggestive remark or two. Undeterred by her silence, the optimist was stepping up his ladykiller tactics. She cut her roast beef and dropped her hand under the table.

She smiled at him winsomely. He leered back at her until he felt something prodding his belly. Uneasily, he dropped his gaze. The something prodding his belly was Hattie's knife.

He eyed her aghast. Gently, she informed him.

'Back in Blitzenberg vere I come from, ve haf a sayink. Ven man puts hand vere he didn't should, Madchen puts knife vere she *did* should.'

The hand was hastily withdrawn.

After lunch, when the showfolk returned to their passenger car, Ella curtly summoned Hattie to her compartment.

'Schmidt. In here.' When Hattie entered, she issued a command and an ultimatum. 'Go back to the dining car and bring me a bottle of brandy, hide it under your dress. Do it *now*, or you're fired.'

'*Bitte*, Madam,' Hattie cheerfully replied. 'I am hired by Herr Shelley. Only Herr Shelley can set fire to me. No schnapps for Madam. You are on der vagon, ja?'

'Damn Max. Well, make yourself useful. Brush my hair.'

'*Mit Vergnugen*, Madam.'

Taking the proffered brush, she went to work, experiencing again the

70

distinctive perfume of Ella's soap. As she brushed the soprano's lustrous hair, she hummed a Strauss waltz. Off-key. Deliberately. Ella grimaced in disgust and threatened to throw her off the train.

The door of the adjoining compartment was open, Rick sitting with Max and Geraldo and keeping an eye on his wife. Also giving Hattie a once-over was dark-eyed Geraldo.

'I got high hopes for Inger,' Max said contentedly. 'Nice girl. Looks strong too, so maybe she's what Ella needs.'

'Smart too,' Rick assured him.

'And — wow!' enthused Geraldo. 'Some shape! A real looker, that kraut babe!'

With an amused grin, Rick challenged him.

'Hey, amico, whatsa datta you say?'

'Me and my big mouth,' sighed Geraldo.

'Come on, Gerry, Rick would've wised up to you sooner or later anyway,' shrugged Max. 'And discretion's his middle name. We can count on him to keep a secret. All friends together here, aren't we?'

'Gerry's as Italian as I'm Arabian,' guessed Rick.

'Getz is the real name,' confided Geraldo.

'The fake Italian bit impresses bookers and audiences,' explained Max. 'And, if you know music, I don't have to convince you he's a great accompanist.'

'No argument,' said Rick. 'One of the best I've heard.'

'Thanks, Rick,' nodded Geraldo. And Rick's amusement increased as the little man removed his glossy wig to mop his brow and cranium. The temples and the sideburns were the genuine article; the whole top part of his head *needed* that toupée. 'And I got to tell you it's a break for me, you joining us. For me, keeping Ella dry has been murder.'

'Gerry's not fooling,' grouched Max. 'Many's the time she's slapped him around. And it's too bad he doesn't always duck fast enough.'

Rick puffed on his cigar and asked, 'They have a theatre at Steeple Rock?'

'No theatre,' said Max. 'It's a farming and mining town. Growing fast, I'm told. We'll be playing the Community Hall.'

'This train arrives five this afternoon,' Geraldo said after checking his watch. 'I just hope Billy's registered us at a decent hotel.'

'I don't think it's a hick town,' said Max. 'Well, I'm betting we'll get a big welcome. Then it'll be supper at the hotel and on to the hall to do the show. Billy'll be in Ibanez by now, setting us up for another one-nighter. But we don't go to Ibanez by train. No railroad to Ibanez, so it has to be a stagecoach journey. Billy's chartered a special coach. Now, Rick, you'll be keeping a sharp eye out . . . '

'Satisfaction guaranteed,' said Rick.

'It's just, some of these towns we play, we can't bar all backstage visitors,' fretted Max. 'Some of 'em could be, you know, civic leaders, the mayor, the banker — important guys. And they're the kind Ella sets her sights on.'

'My eyes'll be busy,' Rick promised.

'Watch 'em like a hawk,' advised Max.

'Ella has her ways,' warned Geraldo. 'Oh, hell, she can be so *cunning*.'

'So can I,' said Rick. 'Just leave everything to me. Better put your hair back on, Gerry. You could catch cold.'

Steeple Rock was ready for the Ella Cardew company. This was evident when, at 5 o'clock that afternoon, the southbound rolled to a halt to the accompaniment of much cheering from a crowd converging on the railroad depot. While Geraldo looked to the unloading of the baggage and its transfer to the hotel, the mayor delivered a speech of welcome to the disembarking showfolk.

Rick and Hattie, scanning the main street, saw ample testimony to Billy Beale's talent as advanceman. Posters bearing Ella's likeness were plastered everywhere, and they easily identified the community hall; it had to be the building festooned with bunting.

The company had been booked into the Belgin Hotel, the best Steeple Rock had to offer. Geraldo, after everybody had been installed in their rooms, produced his toolkit and bee-lined for the hall to check on the piano.

At early supper in the hotel dining room, no liquor was ordered, but Rick wasn't fooled when Ella headed alone for the kitchen, insisting she would inspect it rather than risk ptomaine.

Half-way through the meal, just as Rick anticipated, a smirking waiter placed a carafe of clear liquid and a glass by the star's right hand.

'Hold it a minute,' he ordered. And, while Ella glared at him, he poured from the carafe and took a sip. 'Waiter, take this back. Miss Carew won't be needing it.'

'*I'll* decide what I drink!' she declared.

The waiter supported her. So did

the hotel manager, who materialized to declare that, as far as he was concerned, nothing was too good for the famous Ella Cardew; she had only to ask.

'And I don't doubt the lady asked,' said Rick. Casually, he nudged back the left lapel of his coat, treating the waiter and the manager to a glimpse of his shoulder-holstered .38. 'But we aren't going to get into an argument about it — are we?'

Ella's supporters found Rick's bland grin every bit as intimidating as the little they'd seen of his hardware. Mutually deciding their discretion exceeded their valour, they refrained from further protest and retreated. Ella's eyes flashed. She expressed the hope that, when next he shaved, Rick would cut his jugular.

Max was more appreciative, and profoundly impressed.

'You handled that just fine, Rick. Neat and quiet. No hullabaloo.'

'Herr Buttock is clever, ja?' enthused Hattie.

'Inger, I'll really have to teach you to pronounce my name correctly,' Rick said in mild reproach.

'He's a pain in the . . . ' flared Ella.

'Not so loud,' cautioned Max. 'Remember you're on show all the time and everywhere.'

At 7.45 pm, Ella and company were escorted by the Steeple Rock law officers to the rear door of the community hall. The locals had gone to pains; the dressing room facilities could have been a lot worse.

With the hall jam-packed, the star gowned and made up and Hattie dancing attendance on her, Rick offered encouragement to Max.

'We'll be watching from the wings. Don't worry about anything, friend. Just give the paying customers the spiel, present your star and leave the rest to us.'

'You and Inger?'

'Watching from side stage. On the job, Max. Every minute.'

'Yeah, well, Ella's not the only one you have to watch.'

'As if you need to remind me.'

Max strutted on stage at exactly 8 o'clock and was eagerly applauded by a capacity crowd of locals, miners and farm folk in their Sunday-best. He had to wait a full minute before launching his spiel. The routine was the same, never changed. Geraldo was accorded an ovation which he acknowledged with a convincing show of Latin emotion. Hattie clamped hands to ears when Ella made her entrance.

'They love her,' she remarked to her husband.

When the thunder of applause subsided and Ella began her first song, Hattie drew her hands from her ears and Rick soberly opined,

'They love her looks, honey, and that great voice.'

'The smile that could melt ice,' Hattie added.

'Would they love the woman herself, if they knew her as we do?' mused

Rick. 'Pitiful, isn't it? Face of an angel, disposition of a wildcat.'

'She's getting to you. You're sorry for her.'

'How about you?'

'I guess it's contagious. Yes, I pity her too, but we daren't relax around her, Rick.'

'Not for one minute. Only when she sleeps is she safe from herself.' Rick lightened the mood by commenting. 'In that plain outfit and with your hair braided, you're a peach of a fraulein.'

'Who do you love most?' she good-humouredly challenged. 'Hattie or Inger?'

'Tough question,' he said. 'Give me time to think about it.'

During the interval, Max felt obliged to permit a select group of local men, notables of Steeple Rock, to visit his star in her dressing room. From the open doorway, Rick sized them up. While the mayor, a banker and other civic dignitaries vied for Ella's attention, he noted that the flabby merchant, McWhitty by name and owner of no fewer than three of the town's stores, seemed most in favour with her. The few words that passed between them caused moon-faced McWhitty to beam in eager anticipation. To a detective as intuitive as Rick, this had to be a danger signal; McWhitty was the man to watch.

After interval, with Ella again entertaining her enraptured audience, he confided to Hattie.

'My gut warns me our thirsty thrush has won herself a supplier.'

'For her, that'd be easy,' frowned Hattie. 'Which drooler do you suspect? The jovial banker, the mayor with his diamond stickpin . . . ?'

'My money's on Steeple Rock's most well-heeled merchant. I caught his name. McWhitty.'

'We'll see him again after the show?'

'I'd make book on it, honey. But *she* won't see him.'

'You'll head him off at the pass?'

80

'Specifically, this side of the rear door.'

At the conclusion of the performance, Ella was cheered to the rafters. The stage was pelted with bouquets and gold coins as she took her bows, after which Hattie hurried to the dressing room and stood in readiness to help her change. When Ella entered, she was accompanied by a protesting Max.

'Now, Ella, I can't let you out of my sight, and you know why! Do we have to go all through it again?'

'Like it or not, I've accepted a gentleman's invitation to a late supper,' she retorted en route to a screen. 'I'm hungry again and I just *yearn* to socialize, if only for an hour, and there's nothing you can do about it.'

'Damn it, I'm responsible for . . . ' he began.

'You!' Ella pointed imperiously in Hattie's direction. 'Out!'

Hattie withdrew, leaving the star and her manager still in heated argument, moving to the open door where her husband stood guard.

'You were right,' she softly informed him. 'She's hooked a big fish.'

'And that fish is swimming this way,' he opined, studying his watch. 'Should arrive in one, two, three more seconds and — here he is.'

The merchant appeared in the doorway complete with high hat, bouquet and smug grin. In response to Rick's enquiry, he announced,

'McWhitty's the name. Here to take Miss Cardew to supper, best cafe in town, got a table reserved and . . . '

'I sure admire an optimist,' remarked Rick, returning his grin.

'Well, real privilege for me, big honour, you know?' winked McWhitty. 'This could be quite a party.'

'If it came to pass, friend,' said Rick. 'If it came to pass.'

With that, he slid his left hand to the merchant's inside pocket and withdrew a flat flask of high-grade bourbon. While uncorking it with his teeth, he inserted the index and third finger of his right hand into the waistband of McWhitty's pants and tugged. The uncorked flask was then fitted into the opening bottom-up and McWhitty, frozen and bug-eyed, could only gawk at him. The gawk changed to a wince as the flask emptied, the raw liquor saturating his paunch and everything below it.

Hattie somehow suppressed her mirth. Instead of laughing, she exclaimed,

'*Himmel*! Now dat's *embarrassink*!'

As the merchant retreated in wet pants disorder, Ella emerged from the dressing room, took in the scene at a glance and promptly screamed abuse at her bodyguard, while Max strove to placate her.

'I'll make you regret this, Braddock! I swear you'll end up wishing you'd never laid eyes on me!'

'Can't imagine I'd ever wish that,' Rick said amiably. 'You're always a treat to my eyes, beautiful lady, even when your feathers are ruffled and you're cussing like a bar-room bawd.'

Ella was still in a fury when, in her room at the hotel, Hattie was helping her disrobe and don a nightgown. She needed a whipping boy but, no boy being available, she vented her rage on Hattie.

'Careful, you clumsy kraut bitch! You damn near tore my petticoat!'

Hattie didn't much appreciate having her face slapped. She blinked more in surprise than pain and raised her left hand to her smarting cheek. A little pressure of the fingertips assured her no teeth had been loosened, and now Ella was arrogantly turning her back. Bad timing on her part.

Hattie's hard kick to her cami-knickered derriere drove Ella forward to flop across the bed. She rolled over, rose to a half-sitting position and gaped in shock, as Hattie wagged a reproachful forefinger and told her.

'Back in Blitzenberg ve have a sayink. A slap mit der hand makes face ache, but a foot in the fanny is no fun at all.'

84

'You — you . . . ' The singer was at a loss for words, almost. 'How *dare* you! I'll — tear every hair out of your head!'

'No,' said Hattie. 'You vill get in bed und Inger vill be sleepink in next room mit door und vun eye open.'

Before retiring to the adjoining room, she did a thorough check of the star's quarters, the usual search for secreted liquor.

By the time sleep finally claimed Ella Cardew, she was mentally exhausted from wracking her brain to devise the most harrowing punishment for the indignity inflicted on her by a Nemesis with the face of a guileless fraulein and a kick like a mule's.

★ ★ ★

The company departed Steeple Rock early next morning, packed into a specially chartered stagecoach whose driver was to travel a short cut route to Ibanez and their next engagement; anticipated time of arrival 4 pm of this day. All baggage travelled on the roof or in the boot. The scrawny driver and the nuggety guard were overawed to be transporting the famous Ella Cardew and had said as much, identifying themselves as Clem and Jud respectively. Max promised them free admission to tonight's show, standing room, in return for as easy a run as they could manage; Clem promised to do his best.

Two miles out of Steeple Rock, the showfolk were making no secret of the fact that this was not their favourite mode of travel. Countering Ella's surly complaints, Max stressed the discomfort would prove worthwhile. A packed house guaranteed at the Pellier Theatre in Ibanez, another high profit engagement.

Max was planted on the rear seat with his star between him and Hattie, Rick and Geraldo on the forward seat with a sizeable picnic basket beside them.

The kitchen staff of the Belgin Hotel had been most considerate. Somewhere along the route, the showfolk would need to pause and take lunch alfresco. Geraldo remarked they would not be hungry when they reached their destination. Enough food in the hamper for a good meal for all, including the coach crew.

Rick, scanning the terrain through which the swaying Concord carried them, sighted no homesteads in the distance, not one grazing steer. This was open country. His .38 was snug in its armpit holster, but it paid to be cautious. He resolved, when they made their lunch stop, to break out his Colt .45.

A bump as a wheel dislodged a rock. It shook the vehicle. Ella grimaced angrily, Geraldo swore in Italian, Rick and Hattie traded shrugs and Max waxed apologetic.

'This's no smooth trip, but we oughtn't complain. The idea was to get us to Ibanez the fastest way.'

'It's barbaric!' snapped Ella. 'The least you could have done, the least you owed me, was to arrange an itinerary taking us to towns on the railroad.'

'Told you when we left San Francisco,' he reminded her. 'Not all the rich towns with big populations're on the railroad routes.'

'You're used to it of course,' she sneered at Rick. 'The hardy westerner who can endure *any* discomfort.'

'Like you, I prefer train travel, Miss Cardew,' he drawled. 'Or a good horse under me. Comes to travelling by stage, I just take the rough with the smooth. It's my experience that complaining doesn't help anyway.'

'You okay, Inger?' Max thought to ask.

'Oh ja,' shrugged Hattie. 'Back home in Osterreich, der road to Blitzenberg is *sehr* bompy.'

'Which wouldn't bother coach travellers, I presume,' Ella said caustically. 'Too busy to notice, too busy stuffing themselves with liverwurst, knockwurst and who knows how many other kinds of sausage. Who knows — and who cares?'

'Vell,' smiled Hattie. 'On a bompy ride, is easier to eat sausage dan schnitzel.'

To Max, the star declared in disgust,

'She's so relentlessly cheerful — she makes me sick.'

For an hour or more, conversation lapsed. Max then patted his belly and remarked,

'All that talk of food set an edge to my appetite. I'm thirsty too.'

'Would it be too much to hope the hotel staff included a few bottles when they packed that hamper?' demanded Ella. 'Some decent wine?'

'Too much to hope,' said Rick. 'I took the precaution of warning the chef. But they did include some fresh-ground coffee so, if we stop where there's firewood for the gathering . . . '

'Coffee,' she scowled.

'Easier on the vocal chords than booze,' chided Max. 'Also the diaphragm.'

'How I long to be rid of you killjoys!' she said vehemently.

It was twenty minutes after high noon when the stage forded a creek, a shallow tributary of the Arkansas, the water rising no higher than the wheelhubs. The driver stalled his team a short distance from the bank in what appeared ideal conditions; lush, edible grass for the horses, an oak providing shade for the travellers and ample firewood all around.

First to alight, Rick offered his arm to his wife, then to Ella. Max and Geraldo climbed out to flex cramped limbs and briefly admire the surrounding scenery. The creek sparkled, the brush and grass in this vicinity offered a show of deep green. Away to the west extended wide prairie dotted with sagebrush.

The crew elected to get a fire going and brew coffee. A cloth was spread and, from the basket, Geraldo happily removed cutlery, cups and plates and a fine variety of cold fare; ham, beef and chicken ready-sliced, hardboiled eggs, fresh fruit, a jar of dill pickles, etc.

Lunch was served and the travellers and stage crew ate their fill, Jud the guard keeping an eye on the coffeepots. It would have been a pleasant, relaxing meal but for Ella's sullen demeanour.

Jud poured coffee, offered the first cup to Ella, the second to Hattie and humbly declared he and his partner were 'right proud' to be transporting such fine ladies and friendly gents. Ella eyed him stonily, Hattie rewarded him with a warm smile and Max responded as genially as he could manage.

'I know you guys'll get us to Ibanez on time. We all appreciate that, but . . .'

'That's what the stage line pays us for, Mister Shelley, sir,' said Clem.

' . . . but I just wish,' finished Max, 'you could drive right around those bumps and potholes instead of through them.'

'We're mighty sorry about that,' said Clem. 'The goin's easier along a regular

91

stage trail but, when you're followin'
a short cut, there's always holes and
rocks.'

'Good coffee,' remarked Rick.

'*Sehr gut*,' enthused Hattie.

'*Si*!' agreed Geraldo. '*Bello*!'

'This desolate, dreary country,'
complained Ella. 'God-forsaken and
dangerous. The wild west — who
needs it? No place for a woman.
Wolves, those wailng creatures . . .'

'Coyotes,' offered Rick.

' . . . and Indians.' Ella shuddered.
'Bloodthirsty redskins who could attack
us at any time. We're so vulnerable.
Max Shelley, I'll never forgive you.
Never.'

Clem and Jud swapped glances. The
driver then hastened to put Ella's fears
at rest.

'Why, ma'am, there's scarce any war
parties raidin' travellers nowadays. More
and more Injuns're on reservations,
with the good ol' U.S. Cavalry makin'
sure they stay peaceable.'

'Last Injun trouble I heard of in

Colorado — lemme think now.' Jud scratched his head and shed dandruff. 'Must've been months ago. There was this renegade half-breed they called Bearcat Webster got himself a war party and was makin' a lot of devilry a ways south of here, place called Shayville.'

'Uh huh,' nodded Clem. 'Had a hideaway in the Laberinto Hills. Now that's a *good* long way from here.'

'Momma mia!' flinched Geraldo.

'Oh, Lord,' groaned Ella.

'But nobody needs fret about Bearcat no more,' Jud assured her. 'He's a good renegade now, meanin' a dead'un. And all his braves got captured. Well, you city gents wouldn't've heard about that ruckus, but maybe you?' He eyed Rick. 'From Denver, ain't you? It was writ up in all the newspapers.'

With masterly understatement, and resisting the urge to trade glances with his wife, Rick remarked,

'It does sound kind of familiar.'

Would he or Hattie ever forget Shay

County, the big crisis down there, the tricks they pulled, the risks they took to restore order to Shay County? Their second big case, and dangerous right from the start.

He was remembering his fight to the death with the homicidal Bearcat Webster when he drained his cup, rose and moved to the coach. Climbing to the roof, he managed to remove his Colt from his bag without disturbing the other baggage. That trusty weapon girded his loins when he returned to the fire and reseated himself.

Ella was unaware of his shoulder-holstered .38. She had eyes only for the heavier weapon — worried eyes.

'We're in no danger, or so I'm asked to believe, but it suddenly occurs to you to strap on that pistol,' she frowned.

'Take it easy, Ella,' soothed Max. 'Rick's a westerner and your body-guard. Guys like him don't feel complete unless they're packing a gun. That right, Rick?'

'Just a routine precaution, Miss Ella,' drawled Rick.

The meal over, the travellers relaxed, all but Ella. Clem filled and lit a corncob pipe; the other men smoked cigars offered by Max. It was tranquil here by the creekbank. Max, gazing west, remarked on the moving dust on the horizon. Clem and Jud glanced in the direction and speculated.

'Cattle country over that way. Bunch of cowhands huntin' strays.'

'Uh huh,' grunted Jud. 'Most likely.'

'Must be a hard life for cowhands,' mused Max. 'People like us, city people, wouldn't have any idea how hard.'

'Even when they're part of a well-tended herd, cattle stray,' said Rick. 'Chasing after bunch-quitters goes with the job.'

'Speaking from experience?' challenged Ella.

'I've been a ranch-hand,' he calmly assured her. 'The truth is, Miss Ella, I was many things before I established

95

my detective agency.'

'Jack-of-all-trades?' grinned Max.

'And master of some,' said Rick.

Out of the dust, the riders materialized, six of them.

'Headed our way,' observed Jud.

'Curious?' asked Max.

'Sure,' shrugged Clem. 'Ranch-hands're as curious as any other jaspers. They've seen our smoke. By now, they've sighted the rig. So they'll keep a'comin', and you can scarce blame 'em. Ain't often a cowhand gets to see a lady as purty as Miss Ella up close.'

The six advanced on the party, moving faster now. They were rigged in range clothes, Rick noted. They had the look of ranch-hands but, if they were harmless, why was his sixth sense sounding warning signals?

Just before the horsemen arrived, his eyes met Hattie's. Her expression was as eloquent as his; she might as well have said aloud,

'We'd better be ready for anything.'

4

Cause For Alarm

When the riders reined up to stare at the travellers, both Braddocks at once pegged them as more dangerous than regular ranch-hands. They were as rough a sextet of hard cases as Rick had ever encountered.

One of them sized up the party, leered and remarked,

'Hey now, what've we got here? Rich-lookin' folks is what.'

He drew and cocked a six-shooter as Jud made a move to reach his shotgun.

'Forget it,' another man growled.

'Max, I'll *never* forgive you for *this*!' cried Ella.

The first speaker, obviously the gang's leader, spoke gleefully as his cronies emptied their holsters.

'We done good this mornin', but I'm feelin' greedy. How about you boys?'

The other men eagerly agreed. Menaced by six guns, Rick was ordered to rise and unstrap his Colt, also warned to do that slowly and with great care, no tricks. He had no option but to obey. The two women and the other men obeyed the command to get to their feet. Ella was pallid, badly scared. Hattie chose to appear uncomprehending. Max sweated and Geraldo made it obvious he was no hero. He was pop-eyed, didn't care if the whole damn world knew he was a devout coward.

The boss-thief and another man dismounted.

'Gonna relieve 'em of their wallets, huh?' grinned the horseman covering Rick.

'And anything else worth grabbin',' chuckled his leader, his eyes on Hattie and Ella. 'You two stand clear of the men, hear? I — uh — might just want to search you personal.'

'I should never have left San Francisco!' wailed Ella, and almost swooned.

Rick was standing close enough to Max and Geraldo to prepare them without the bandits overhearing. Bandits they had to be, he decided. The saddlebags on those horses bulged. As well, a sack hung from the boss-thief's horse. Not provisions, he was thinking. Cash. A lot of it.

'Be ready to drop — fast — and keep your heads down.'

Never in a million years, he realized, would Hattie allow those rogues to touch Ella, and certainly not herself. This she ensured by distracting all six bandits in her own special way. They gawked at her as, smiling coyly, she bent, took hold of the bottom of her skirt and began raising it, displaying a pair of legs guaranteed to win the attention of all males present. The boss-thief and his companion jerked to a halt incredulously.

Nobody was ready for that most impressive of all distractions, nor for

Hattie's next move. From the tiny holster attached to her right garter, she drew and discharged her Remington derringer. Max and Gerald dropped flat on their faces. Ella stood petrified.

The first slug nicked a horseman's unwashed neck, causing him to loose a startled yelp. The second seared a horse's rump; the animal promptly reared, neighing shrilly and throwing its rider.

Taking advantage of this confusion, Rick whisked his .38 from under his coat and inflicted a leg wound on one of the two who had dismounted. The other, the boss-thief, whirled to draw a bead on him. To save his life, he couldn't risk aiming to wound; his second bullet struck the boss-thief dead centre.

Jud shoved the women to the ground and, from a prone position, grabbed for his shotgun, cocked both barrels and fired, blowing a man out of his saddle.

The bandits' horses were milling,

agitated, when Rick tossed his .38 to Clem, dropped and planted his left hand on his fallen holster, drawing his Colt with his right. The driver caught the Smith & Wesson deftly. The two still active horsemen began shooting, but missed. Clem didn't, neither did Rick, and the fifth and sixth horses were suddenly riderless.

Reloading his shotgun, Jud growled, 'That makes all six of 'em.'

'Keep 'em covered,' urged Rick, recocking his Colt. He moved forward to check on the fallen and kick their pistols clear. A brief inspection. Then, 'All right, friends, it's all over. But, before you pick yourselves up, I'd better prepare you. We have three wounded and three dead men on our hands.'

Hattie still held her garter gun. As she helped Ella upright, she murmured reassuringly,

'Ve safe now, madam. No more boomink mit der guns.'

And no response from a temporarily speechless Ella. Max and Geraldo

101

struggled upright to gape in shock at the fallen, only the man with the leg wound audible, cursing in agony. The one thrown by his horse had gone to ground head-first and was out cold. Just as unconscious was the one shot by Clem, sprawled on his back, bleeding from his right shoulder. The boss-thief and the other two were as dead as they would ever be.

'Hell's bells!' breathed Max.

'Clem and Jud owe you no apology, nor do I, but I'm sure we're sorry,' muttered Rick. 'Quite an ordeal for you folks. Just don't assume it happens all the time, okay? This was unexpected, something none of us could foresee.'

'Outlaws,' said Max, swallowing a lump in his throat.

'Well,' said Rick. 'It's for sure they aren't just fun-loving cowboys on a spree.' He moved to a horse, raised the flap of a saddlebag, thrust a hand in and withdrew it to exhibit a fistful of banknotes. 'Clem, Jud, you know the stage routes hereabouts. What's your guess?'

'I wouldn't reckon they held up a stage,' frowned Clem.

'I'm guessing a bank,' said Rick.

'Whatta we gotta do?' fretted Geraldo. 'Digga da graves, bury thema?'

'And what do we do about the three still breathing?' wondered Max. 'Look, Rick, we sure owe you — but — I don't want to sound callous — we're booked to play Ibanez tonight.'

Rick restored the cash to the saddle-bag and stared westward.

'Look where I'm looking, Max,' he invited. 'You could see dust again. The bank had to be in a township. When a bank's robbed, lawmen don't sit on their hands and say 'Gee, what a tough break.' They do something about it. They deputize a posse and hunt the robbers. And, the way this bunch crossed the flatland, it didn't look to me they were trying to kill their backtrail. I don't think they were smart enough to do that. They were a dangerous outfit, but not all that smart.'

The driver returned Rick's .38 and declared,

'I swear I didn't believe we had any kinda chance.'

'Me too,' said Jud. 'They had the drop on us. If it wasn't for what *she* did . . . '

He turned to stare at Hattie. So did the other men. She had persuaded Ella to sit and rest and was now raising her skirts to re-secrete her tiny pistol; this time she did it with her back turned to one and all.

'Damn it, Rick, you guaranteed she's reliable, but I'd never've believed she was carrying a gun,' said a profoundly impressed Max. 'Or *where* she carries it.'

'It's supposed to be a *concealed* weapon after all,' shrugged Rick.

'She'sa fulla surprises,' mumbled Geraldo.

'*Must* be experienced,' frowned Max.

'That's our Inger,' nodded Rick. 'I

imagine there's many a tale she could tell — from the Vienna woods.'

Hattie turned to face them again, smiling cheerily. Max stared to the west and proved he was developing a talent for sighting distant dust. Clem and Jud had seen it too.

'Bigger party,' opined Clem.

'Probably a posse,' said Rick. 'Too bad about the delay, but whoever's in charge rates an explanation. Even so, we mightn't be all that late getting into Ibanez. What do you say, Clem?'

'Let's see now,' mused the driver. 'If we didn't get raided, we'd be leavin' round now. Uh huh. Might make it a half-hour later'n schedule. Depends how much jawin' there's gonna be.'

Rick counted nine riders approaching across the flats. While waiting for them, he ejected spent shells, reloaded his weapons and strapped on the Colt. Then he lit another cigar.

The nine riders came on fast and reined up to survey the scene of carnage. A posse for sure. The scrawny man with the young-old face and moody eyes wore a star. He identified himself as Bob Hedge, a deputy sheriff of Regan County.

'The Sackett bunch — what's left of 'em,' he observed. 'They looted the McCloud Mercantile Bank at Regansville, the county seat.'

'That much I guessed after the excitement was over,' offered Rick. 'I checked a saddlebag. The cash was just stuffed into it. Braddock's my name. I'm a private detective.' He introduced the troupe and stage crew and named their destination, adding, 'This is an unfortunate delay, frightening for Miss Cardew, as you'll appreciate.'

He need not have identified the famous soprano. Hedge's volunteers obviously recognized her; they weren't looking at anybody else.

'All right, they tried to make trouble with you people and any fool can see there was a shootout and they got the worst of it,' said the deputy. 'If you want to save time, you do all

106

the talkin.' That way, I won't have to question your whole party.'

Rick summarized it for him, a full account of the incident, but terse, no rambling. Hedge had only one question for the other travellers. Had it all happened exactly as Mr Braddock had explained?

'That's how it was,' nodded Clem. 'Just like he told it.'

'Good enough for me,' decided Hedge. 'You folks're free to pack up and get rollin' again. We'll take care of the losers, use your fire to fix us some coffee, doctor them that're hurtin' and take 'em to the Regan County jail along with the three stiffs.'

Every word uttered by Rick and the lawman was repugnant to Ella Carew, the matter-of-fact, no-nonsense summary of an outlaw gang's violent and bloody end.

Geraldo repacked the picnic basket, Clem and Jud climbed to the seat and the showfolk reboarded the coach. As the vehicle moved off, Ella's accompanist glanced out a window and glimpsed a couple of possemen lifting a dead bandit, draping the body across a horse. He shuddered.

Max mopped his brow, exhaled noisily and addressed his star.

'You got an apology coming, Ella. The whole thing must've been a nightmare for you. On the other hand, it *was* unexpected. None of us would ever have guessed . . . '

'In my entire career . . . ' She found her voice again. And used it, 'in my whole life — I have never been so terrified! Those fiends would have — laid their filthy hands on me . . . '

'No chance,' Rick said calmly.

'No chance?' She glared at him. 'You! Always so sure of everything!'

'I thought you understood, Miss Ella,' he said, gesturing to his wife. 'Inger isn't just your dresser and maid. She's your second bodyguard. Any badman tries to harm you, she protects you. Proved it, didn't she?'

'I was frozen in shock!' gasped Ella.

'I still don't know how this — this bovine Brunhild — could arm herself with — that ridiculous little pistol!'

'Those derringers're certainly small,' drawled Rick. 'They carry only two bullets which don't have much impact. But, at short range, they're fairly effective. What we needed was a diversion, something to throw those bandits off guard. Inger provided that diversion.' He accorded his wife an approving nod. 'Good girl, Inger.'

'*Dankeschon, Herr* Buttock,' beamed Hattie.

'Braddock,' he corrected.

'Well, *I* saw where she pulled that gun from,' Max said eagerly. 'And, holy Toledo, this Fritz kid's quick on the drawers.'

'Quick on the draw,' winced Rick.

'Sorry,' said Max. 'No offence, Inger.'

'Heaven preserve me!' groaned Ella. 'She keeps a pistol in her underwear?'

'Dis is der Vild Vest, madam,' shrugged Hattie.

'It was a ghastly experience, just ghastly,' complained Ella. 'My nerves are in shreds. Brandy, Max. I couldn't possibly perform tonight in my present condition. I need something to settle my nerves.'

Max shook his head emphatically.

'Never try to fool your manager,' he chided. 'It was rough on you, rough on all of us, but you're a trouper, Ella, a real pro. We both know you'll knock 'em dead at the Pellier Theatre tonight.'

'I'll be incapable of . . . ' began Ella.

'You vill feel fine,' Hattie promised. 'Inger vill take care of you, give you massage . . . '

'Don't even *think* of it!' retorted Ella. 'Pummelled by those Teutonic paws, I'd be crippled! I'd totter on stage aching all over!'

'So no massage,' said Max. 'But you'll be a big hit, Ella. You'll be just great. Just keep thinking of all that applause — and your fat share of the box office take.'

Ella eyed Rick again.

'I have a vague recollection of something you said back there,' she frowned. 'Three dead, three wounded?'

'I did say that,' he nodded.

'And so calmly,' she accused.

'You're assuming I have little respect for human life?' he challenged.

'I would say that's all too obvious,' she replied.

'There's a lot you don't understand, probably don't *want* to understand,' he told her. 'I do respect human life, but we're entitled to proper concern for our own lives. Self defence is every man's right. Our driver and guard — and I — had to make every shot count, and don't forget we were all under threat, protecting not just ourselves, but you, Max and Gerry — and Inger, whose pistol was empty by that time. You saw some killing today, but . . . '

'Easy, Rick,' begged Max. 'Eaz-eee.'

'But who deserved to be shot?' Rick finished relentlessly. 'The bandits

111

attacking us, or some of us — you, for instance?'

Ella insisted on the last word.

'This frontier country,' she said bitterly, 'is no place for civilized people.'

★ ★ ★

They rolled into the main street of Ibanez at 4.40 pm. Another noisy welcome. Ibanez boasted a brass band exceeding in volume the cheers of the citizenry. By the time they were alighting from the coach in front of the Hotel de Paris, located conveniently close to Pellier's Theatre, Rick suspected those enthusiastic musicians knew only one tune. Well, they blared that same tune over and over.

Again, Billy Beale had paved the way for them. No need for Rick to negotiate with local law officers for safe escort of the company from the hotel to the theatre; Billy had arranged that. Their hotel accommodation was satisfactory as far as everybody but Rick was concerned. The star and her dresser would be in side by side single bedrooms, but there was no connecting door. He decided extra precautions should be taken this night.

Over supper, Max expected a show of gratitude from his star.

'This town's doing you proud,' he enthused. 'How about that great bedroom? You couldn't be more comfortable back in 'Frisco. Well, it doesn't overlook the main street, sure, but a rear room's always quieter, no traffic noise to bother you.'

'You sleep *gut* tonight, Madam,' Hattie said encouragingly.

'After giving a performance Ibanez'll remember for years to come,' offered Rick.

'Ho fame,' grinned Geraldo, cutting into his steak.

In better Italian than he could ever manage, Ella curtly retorted.

'*Ho sete.*'

'You're thirsty,' Rick translated.

'Gerry's hungry, you're thirsty.'

'So you know a little Italian,' she acknowledged. 'But you're still ignorant. You certainly *don't* know how to please a woman.'

'I know what's good for some women and what's not so good for others,' he calmly assured her. 'And, for you, liquor is bad medicine.'

'I'm an individual, damn it,' she snapped. 'And sick and tired of everybody else claiming they know what's best for me. You two . . .' She glared at Max and Geraldo, 'and now the hired help.'

'Eat your supper,' urged Max. 'A hungry soprano doesn't need gin, Ella, but she sure needs nourishment.'

Local lawmen got Ella and her retinue to the theatre with time to spare. She was gawked at and applauded, but the locals kept their distance. The effusive Leo Pellier made a ceremony of conducting them to a dressing room which, however grudgingly, the star had to admit was to her taste.

While Hattie helped her change and the theatre filled, Max talked business with Pellier, Geraldo checked the piano and Rick made his usual scout of the backstage facilities.

It would happen again here; he was in no doubt about that. Well-heeled friends of the theatre owner, local big shots, would be presented to Ella during the intermission. What strategy would she resort to this time? he wondered. Well, she could forget about an after the show *tête-à-tête* with an Ibanez admirer.

If she remembered her bodyguard's effective dismissal of Citizen McWhitty of Steeple Rock.

He could be certain of only one thing. If only to defy her manager, to see Max suffering more agitation than was good for him, she would devise *some* scheme. This was her way and, by now, Rick was well and truly wise to her ways; he would be as vigilant as ever.

The recital began on schedule and

to another packed house, Max's grand introduction, Geraldo with his wig firmly settled and his flashing smile a fixture, Ella making her entrance to deafening applause. As always, the audience applauded her first song and every ballad and aria of the first half.

At interval, an even more impressive group of leading citizens than the Steeple Rock big shots socialized with the star in her dressing room, with Rick and Hattie sizing them up and quietly speculating.

'The banker's making a big play for her,' Hattie observed. 'That smile of hers could start him drooling any moment. I think he'd forget his family ever existed, do *anything* for her.'

'I'm glad our cash is in a Denver bank,' muttered Rick. 'If he's hot to impress her, he probably wouldn't draw the line at embezzlement of his bank's funds.'

'Of that whole heavy-breathing half-dozen,' said Hattie, 'which one do you guess is the likeliest contender?'

'My money's on tall, dark and handsome with the diamond stickpin — another diamond on his pinkie,' said Rick. 'He was introduced as Diamond Jack Vernon. I noticed his place of business when we were rolling into town, couldn't miss it, biggest and fanciest saloon in Ibanez.'

'You could be right about him.'

'If I'm right, I'm also curious. What kind of trick will she pull this time? Well, we'll see.'

The second half of the programme obviously lived up to the expectations of Ibanez folk who had paid considerably more than nickels and dimes to see and hear a celebrity artiste perform. No fewer than five curtain calls for Ella, plus tumultuous applause and several over-stimulated males forcibly restrained from climbing onto the stage. With queenly demeanour, Ella acknowledged such feverish gestures as no more than her due.

Backstage after the show, much to the surprise of Hattie, Max and then

Rick, no mention from the star of admirers inviting her to a late supper.

'I'm exhausted, utterly exhausted,' she complained, and stifled a yawn. 'So many encores.'

'You were a smash, honey,' beamed Max.

'Not since Edwin Booth's 'Hamlet' in this theatre, Miss Cardew,' declared Pellier, 'has there been such an ovation.'

'*Magnifico!*' Geraldo kissed his fingertips.

'Take me to the hotel,' begged Ella. 'I need sleep — so desperately.'

Max bought that, but the look exchanged by the Braddocks was eloquent. Translation: 'Who does she think she's kidding?'

The Ibanez law officers did their duty again. Under escort, the company returned to the hotel. Max and Geraldo retired to their rooms, Hattie helped Ella remove her makeup and prepare for bed, after which she fine tooth-combed the room as usual.

'Water in the pitcher and the bedside

carafe,' she reported to her husband before retiring to her own room. 'Nary a bottle in there, my love. I searched the dresser, looked under the mattress, checked the commode — everything. And you have suspicion written all over your handsome face.'

'I trust her about as much as you do,' he said.

'So you don't trust her at all.'

'Let that be my problem, sweetheart. No reason you shouldn't call it a day. But not me. Not yet. I plan on taking a look around before I hit the feathers. See you for breakfast.'

Rick descended to the lobby and relaxed in an upholstered chair for as long as it took him to smoke a cigar, then made his exit by way of the street entrance to begin his scout.

The alley on the hotel's north side was no narrow cut-off; more a side street than an alley. Strolling it toward the rear of the building, he passed a tethered horse. Though he spared the animal only a casual glance, he assumed it belonged to a ranch-hand of this territory; the coiled lariat made that obvious.

Little if any moonlight tonight, so the area back of the hotel, most of it anyway, was shrouded in gloom. He moved around quietly, noting points of potential importance, Ella's second floor window and balcony, shrubbery in the rear yard and a lone tree. A dead tree, thanks to termites or for whatever reason. And tall, already bereft of foliage, its limbs littering the ground, all but the thick one jutting toward the back wall. Very remiss of the hotel manager, he reflected. The tree should have been cut down and removed long before now.

He lounged by the corner, waiting patiently, listening for some ten minutes. Then he heard the furtive footsteps, glimpsed the approaching man — toting a ladder no less — and guessed his identity.

Diamond Jack and a ladder, plus no doubt a bottle or two. You had to hand it to Ella. The gal was just full of tricks.

'You and me both, pretty lady,' he was thinking, as he retreated into the alley.

The cowhand's horse was still there.

'Just a loan,' he whispered to it, and detached the coiled lariat.

By the time he returned to the corner, the wealthy saloon-keeper had set the ladder in position and was about to begin his ascent. Skulking into the screening bushes, Rick noted the top of the ladder was resting against the rail of a balcony. Whose balcony? Superfluous question.

He made his way to the tree and was shinning up the trunk to reach the bare branch when lamplight shafted out from Ella's window. She opened it and stepped onto the balcony. Rick darted a glance in that direction and continued his climb to straddle the limb and inch along it, uncoiling his rope. Her blonde hair hung loose. She was wearing a negligee and smiling down at Diamond

Jack, beckoning eagerly, and he moving toward her rung by rung.

'Romeo and Juliet,' mused Rick, loosening the loop. 'Well, an improvised version thereof.'

Some five feet from his goal, Diamond Jack paused to exhibit a bottle for Ella's appraisal. In ecstasy, she clasped her hands to her bosom. Simultaneously, Rick twirled his loop expertly and made his throw. Devastating accuracy. It fell neatly over the uprights of the ladder, startling Ella. He tugged to tighten it, the line became taut and then he was hauling back on it and Diamond Jack became suddenly apprehensive.

The ladder, with the saloonkeeper clinging to it, parted company with the balcony rail and, for a few moments, was perpendicular. For good reason, Diamond Jack was confused and not a little alarmed. Rick, hoping the branch wouldn't break under his weight, exerted all his strength, hauling relentlessly. To the accompaniment of its occupant's shocked gasp, the ladder keeled backward and hit the dust with a thud and the unmistakable sound of breaking glass. Rick winced as he began climbing down. A cloudbank rolled away from the face of the moon and he was recognized by his sworn enemy.

'You bastard, Braddock!' cried Ella.

She withdrew into her room. The window was closed, the lamp extinguished. Rick dropped and, while detaching the loop and recoiling the rope, sympathized with the man shoving himself clear of the ladder.

'Break anything, Jack?' he asked. 'I mean beside the booze?'

Diamond Jack indicated his bones were undamaged by lurching upright. He was steady on his feet and flexing his muscles; he also winced a lot.

'Hell of a thing to do to a man!' he fumed. 'Half of my ass feels like it's on fire. I had a flask of genuine French cognac in my hip pocket.'

'Mighty unfortunate,' said Rick. 'If you're armed, you oughtn't think of drawing on me. A burning butt'll slow a man down every time.'

'I need a doctor — and an explanation. Why in blue blazes did you do it?'

'Just between us, the hard stuff's bad for her breath control and the tonal quality of that great voice, but she just won't believe it.'

'Who the hell are you anyway?'

'They call me The Lone Lariat.'

'Very funny. Damn! I hate this humiliation, just *hate* it. I'm gonna have to wake up Doc Stewart and have him pull glass out of my ass and he'll laugh all the time. The hell of it is he's like you — a comedian.'

'Try to be brave, Jack. Chances are he'll have to use iodine.'

'Just what I *don't* need!'

With that, Diamond Jack Vernon walked away, his gait awkward, and Rick ambled back to the alley to return the lariat, its owner now standing by his mount, a bow-legged cowboy some five feet five inches tall; if he had a nickname, it had to be Shorty.

'That's my rope!' he exclaimed.

'And now I'm returning it, friend,' said Rick. 'After thinking it over, I changed my mind.'

'About what?' The cowhand was inquisitive.

'I was thinking of hanging myself,' explained Rick. 'But what the hell, suicide won't solve my problems. Coward's way out. I've decided I can endure the pain — maybe for a few more years.'

'You got a sickness?'

'I'm an egocentric. Doctors have warned me there's no cure.'

The cowhand nervously backstepped two paces.

'Is it — uh — catchin'?'

'No. Not contagious. Cowhands never suffer from it. Only in government circles does it become a plague.'

Much relieved, the cowhand swung into his saddle and made himself scarce, leaving Rick just as relieved, confident Ella Cardew would not wake with a raging hangover and that the Braddock

Detective Agency was honouring one of its mottoes — Satisfaction Guaranteed. He re-entered the hotel, climbed to his room and retired, still satisfied, but by no means complacent. Surveillance would have to be maintained.

At the start, it had been a contest, Ella versus Max, she stopping at nothing to defy and harass her manager. It had then become Ella versus the Braddocks, neither of whom would sell her short.

★ ★ ★

This night, while the showfolk slept in Ibanez, Noah Gannon hunkered in a patch of brush with his horse well concealed. His thick jacket and a blanket were his protection against the after-midnight chill.

He was staring far to the south. So distant was the pin-point of light he had barely discerned it, but he was in no doubt. The glow of a campfire, nothing surer. His quarry? Strong possibility.

For days he had bird-dogged the tracks of five horsemen. The provisions packed by his sister had been used up; he was living off the land now.

Patience. And caution. He had reserves of patience and, from the beginning of his quest, had made his every move with the utmost caution. Eventually his efforts would be rewarded, but it would have to be in the right place and at the right time. After every coup, the five deadly shadows had proved themselves past masters in the art of the fast disappearing trick. And one of them, if not all five of them, knew how to kill their backtrail. Tracking these men was the most difficult, most frustrating and time-consuming task Gannon had ever undertaken. But, for three good reasons, he would never quit.

First reason. These predators had kidnapped and ill-treated his son.

Second reason. He needed to retrieve $10,000. Why delude himself? It could take him, his sister and brother-in-law the rest of their lives to repay the bank loan unless, by some miracle, the Deansburg population suddenly doubled and the store became a high profit concern. Which didn't seem likely.

Third reason. And the most important. He had his own problems, but also a deep-rooted regard for the welfare of his fellow-men, certainly those who were law-abiding. Unless they were exposed and captured, those conscienceless killers would stay in business; others would suffer, would lose their savings or their loved ones. A lot of people were in for a lot of grief.

'Wait it out and stay after them,' he urged himself. 'No matter how long it takes to run them to ground.'

He decided he should sleep now. In the morning, hugging all the cover he could find, he would move on to where he had sighted that far distant pinpoint of light.

5

The Eyes of Jethro Smith

Next morning, the chartered stagecoach rolled out of Ibanez with no passengers aboard, just Clem and Jud on the driver's seat, both in good spirits after last night's treat, Ella Cardew's big success at Pellier's Theatre.

During breakfast, Ella had uttered not a word to Rick. However, if looks could kill, he would have expired before digging into his bacon and eggs. Max was in good spirits, the Ibanez engagement having netted a high profit. Geraldo paid Ella a compliment which she shrugged off; last night she had performed superbly.

In a vain attempt to break through the wall of hostility she had built between them, Rick warmly agreed.

'Stroke of genius, including that

aria from 'Madam Butterfly' in your repertoire, Miss Cardew. Most sopranos need a full orchestral backing for that piece but, to just Gerry's accompaniment, you put it over beautifully.'

'Third number after intermission, just the right spot for it,' grinned Max. 'My idea.'

'A perfect rendition,' declared Rick.

Not till they were boarding the train did Ella deign to address him.

'So now you're a music critic?'

'That was a compliment,' said Rick. 'Not criticism.'

This southbound provided all the refinements of the train on which the company had left Denver. They would be accommodated in a Pullman car, the star in a private compartment, her manager and accompanist sharing the adjoining compartment, Rick and Hattie sharing the seat opposite the door to Ella's quarters. The train would move a few minutes from now. Meanwhile, Ella stood in the doorway, eyeing Rick sceptically.

'And just what,' she challenged, 'would a paid snooper know about 'Madam Butterfly' or any other opera?'

'I can draw a comparison — in your favour,' he offered. 'You and Montelli.'

'*Maria* Montelli?' blinked Geraldo.

'The great diva herself,' nodded Rick. 'Two years ago. The San Francisco Opera House. Montelli as Madam Butterfly. As I recall, I treated myself to a seat on the aisle seventh row from the orchestra pit.'

'That'sa gotta be an experience you don'ta forget,' Geraldo said reverently.

'Well, what do you say, Rick?' demanded Max. 'How does Ella stack up against Montelli?'

'What do you want, Max?' Rick asked with a wry grin. 'My honest opinion, or flattery?'

'Give it to me straight,' begged Max.

'Never mind what Max thinks,' ordered Ella. 'Look *me* in the eye and tell me.'

'All right,' shrugged Rick. 'Montelli

hitting High C wavers just a little. You don't. You hit all your high notes with greater clarity.'

The whistle blew. As the train began moving, Ella crooked a finger.

'In here, Braddock.'

She withdrew into her compartment, Max and Geraldo moved along to theirs and, just before Rick began moving, he felt his wife's hand on his arm.

'*Herr* Braddock, *bitte*?'

'Yes, Inger?' he asked.

For his ears alone, she warned.

'If that woman tries to seduce you, we'll have to pull out of this assignment. I swear I'll kick her bustle from one end of this car to the other.'

'It'd be damn near worth it to see that happen,' he whispered.

He entered the compartment, closed the door, seated himself opposite Ella and removed his hat. She complained, while surveying him warily,

'I don't like surprises. I can read

Max and Gerry like an open book, but you're different. As far as I'm concerned, that's a black mark against you. You're too unpredictable for my liking.'

'So we're two of a kind,' he suggested. 'Both of us devious.'

'If you think I'm flattered by all that flim flam — comparing me to Maria Montelli . . . '

'It wasn't flattery. I have a keen ear. I meant what I said about her high notes, hers and yours. Beautiful woman, Montelli, but running to fat. You aren't — yet. Well, too much pasta, too much vino — that's the way it goes, you know?'

'Leave my figure out of this.'

'Can't do that, Miss Cardew. Your voice is your fortune, so is your face, so is your figure, and I'm being paid to protect the whole baggage. Sorry. Wrong word. The whole beautiful package.'

'You bother me, Braddock. Always one jump ahead. And full of tricks.'

'I think we've had this conversation before.'

'Last night, I'd arranged something, and you baulked me again.'

'Just doing my duty, Miss Cardew. You gave me no choice but to discourage Diamond Jack. He's none the worse for the experience, should make a slow but steady recovery. He'll just have to use extra cushions for a while.'

'How did you learn to throw a rope so accurately?'

'Practice makes perfect. I wasn't always a private detective.'

'No? Go ahead. Impress me.'

'Mine has been a chequered career.' Rick wasn't about to go into lengthy detail for the singer's benefit; a summary was all she rated in his book. 'Restless spirits acquire a certain versatility. I've worked cattle, prospected and, if you haven't already noticed, I'm comfortable with showfolk. That's because I've paid my dues, everything from spruiking in carny shows, trick shooting, stage managing travelling theatre groups, a little acting on the side — you name it.'

'I might've guessed you've been a sideshow barker,' she said sourly. 'You with your gift of the gab.'

'I'm not always glib, lady,' he earnestly assured her. 'It comes from the heart, my plea for you to forget the hard stuff for the sake of your health, your career — and your looks.'

'Now you're boring me again,' she complained. 'That's all, Braddock. This conversation just ended.'

He rejoined Hattie.

'Talk,' she ordered.

'Nothing new,' he shrugged. 'Except that she's becoming curious about my background. I'm full of tricks, she says.'

'I could've told her that,' said Hattie.

'*You* could,' he agreed. 'But Inger couldn't.'

'I'm surprised her perfume hasn't brought you out in a rash by now.'

'Oh, that soap she uses? You get

closer to her than I do, so we'd better hope it won't make your eyes water or affect your breathing.'

They could discuss it this casually, the distinctive aroma of the star's favourite soap. At this time, there was no way they could foresee its future significance.

Hattie remarked.

'I don't mind it really. It's a beautiful fragrance when you get used to it. But — holy Mother Murphy — so *strong*!'

★ ★ ★

It was 10 am when Gannon reached the source of the pin-point of light that had won his attention in the hours of darkness. At least he hoped this was the place, this timbered shelf three quarter's of the way up a not too steep mountainside.

He dismounted and tethered the black with extra care, ensuring its movements were restricted. What he did not need right now was for his or any other animal to blot out the possibly significant sign. He stood by his horse a while, head bowed, eyes searching the shelf's floor for disturbed earth, a used match, the morning sun glinting off a half-buried bottle, anything to indicate his quarry. No sign at all, so he began moving around gingerly.

He found no half-burned twigs, no faggots, but he was learning persistence, a useful ally of his patience. With a stick, he began moving earth, prodding, sifting. Then, on his knees, he took up a handful and inspected it closely, noting traces of grey in the dull yellow.

He kept digging, scooping earth away until he found the proof he sought, first one blackened stick that crumbled in his grasp. It was charcoal now; last night it had been firewood. Several more pieces of the same, then more of that powdery grey, ash for sure. All right, he was making progress, but not much.

'Be quite a time before I get close,' he reflected.

Where to from here? Think about that. Having camped this high up the mountainside, would they make the long descent to ride all the way around its base? He doubted that. It seemed more likely they would climb again, save time by going on upward, always assuming the far slope was as gentle as the near one he and they had scaled.

His next move was to prowl the inner edge of the shelf and study the upper slope of the mountain face. And, soon, his diligence was rewarded. Those grooves had to have been dug by the hooves of climbing horses.

Striding back to his horse, he untied it and swung into the saddle. He hustled it across the ledge and put it to the slope for a not too hasty ascent. Much depended on keeping the animal's strength up; a rider could not get far on a winded mount. He let it climb at its own pace and, some time later, they were crossing its woody summit. Prints of the five horses were not so clear now, not until he reined up at the south side and dropped his gaze. The downslant was thick-timbered and dotted with mountain brush and clumps of rock, but he noted other indentations before scanning the area further south.

Lonesome-looking country, undulating terrain marked by rockmounds, straggling columbine, stands of aspen and a copse or two of heavier trees. He could see for a great distance, but was not so optimistic as to hope for a glimpse of horsemen on the move.

It was nearing noon when the long descent ended. He pressed on, but slowly, his gaze on the ground. They were doing it again, he mused. Killing their backtrail, and skillfully. So be it. He would take a chance, push on southward on the assumption they had done likewise.

Sighting the wisp of smoke, he cautiously slowed his mount to a walk and dropped hand to holster. A noon campfire for sure. And on open ground. Whoever had built that fire was making no effort to avoid detection. He rode another mile, relaxing now, doubting one of the five was going it alone. The man was soon clearly visible to him, could see him coming and didn't seem to care. As he drew closer, Gannon observed he was no youngster. Long grey hair straggled from under the brim of a sweat-stained, low-crowned felt hat. That tile had seen better days; so had its owner.

Hunkered by his fire, he looked to be of stocky build and durable for his years, the face lined and sporting a five-day stubble as grey as the long hair. He was roasting jack-rabbit meat and watching a black coffeepot. Without raising his head, he acknowledged the mounted man.

'Howdy. Want to light and set?'

'Obliged,' said Gannon.

Arriving, he dismounted and ground-reined the black beside the shabby oldtimer's animal, a placid buckskin of indeterminate age. The old man had unsaddled it. Beside it were heaped his few possessions, which included a pickaxe and spade.

'Name's Jethro Smith,' he offered.

'Noah Gannon.'

'Plenty meat for the both of us.'

'Thanks. If you got a pan, I'll contribute a can of beans.'

'I got a pan. And beans'll go fine.'

As well as the beans, Gannon broke out a tin plate and cup and a fork. While eating, they talked.

'Prospector,' observed Gannon.

'That's what I am nowadays,' nodded Smith. 'No luck yet, but I'm headed west. Heard tell of a new strike a ways north of the Gunnison River. You on the drift, huh? Cowhand from the looks of you. Figurin' to find a rancher that's hirin'?'

'Used to be a ranch-hand. I help run a store now. Town called Deansburg. Long way from here.'

'You'll be headed back there when

you've found them you're huntin',
I'spect.'

Gannon chewed and swallowed and
fixed a challenging eye on Jethro Smith.
If not a mind reader, this old fossicker
was quite a guesser.

'Jethro, how can you know I'm
hunting?' he demanded.

'You're huntin'.' Smith said it
emphatically. 'Not deer nor quail nor
any critter you'd want to eat. Men.
And you ain't about to quit neither,
gonna stay after 'em. I don't see no
badge, so you ain't no lawman. But
you're sure as hell man-huntin'.'

'All right, but how could you figure
that?'

'The way you come down off of
that mountain, the way you read sign
— or tried to — 'fore you headed for
my fire.'

'For an old prospector, you got keen
eyes.'

'These old ears don't fail me neither,
son. You weren't always a ranch-hand
nor me a prospector. Only been lookin'

142

for gold these past five years. 'Fore that, I was a long time with the cavalry, Colonel Marrigan's regiment.'

'Army scout?'

'Sure enough. Ain't braggin', but ol' Mace Marrigan used to call me the best tracker in all Colorado or anyplace else. I've run 'em all to ground, son, every kinda two-legged varmint you could name, gun-runners, renegade Injuns, troopers that got 'emselves lost, lowdown whites peddlin' rotgut liquor to Arapahos and Pawnees.'

Gannon had warmed to this gnarled old veteran. He didn't hesitate to confide,

'There are five men I have to find.'

'Uh huh,' grunted Smith. 'Well, they're headed south.'

'You sighted . . . ?' Gannon began eagerly.

'Ain't seen hide nor hair of 'em.'

'Then — how do you know . . . ?'

'Cut their sign few hours back. One thing I can tell you, but I guess you've learned it already. They ain't lookin' for company, cover their backtrail good.'

'So — you noticed signs I'd miss.'

'Used to be a cowhand you say. Cowhands savvy trackin' strayed stock. Got to chase rustlers sometimes, huh? So you can follow sign passable good.'

'Not as good as you, Jethro.'

'Reckon not. And it'd take quite a time for me to learn you all I know. A lot of months, son, not just weeks.'

'The hell of it is I don't have that kind of time.'

'Already guessed that. Wanta tell me why you're huntin' 'em? You don't have to if it's none of my business.'

'Just between us?'

'If that's how you want it.'

By the time they were through eating, Gannon had enlightened the old man, imparting all he knew of the professional kidnappers, all he'd learned from bitter personal experience. Jethro Smith listened attentively, offering no comment until he had unburdened himself. Then *he* talked, and decisively.

'It better be done your way, son.

144

Makes sense, what you say. Tell nothin' to no lawman or newspaper feller till you know where they're at.'

Gannon gratefully accepted his offer. He would accompany Smith to where he had cut sign of the five. And do a lot of listening. From now till sundown, when they would go their separate ways, he would strive to absorb all the tracker's lore his tutor would instil in him.

So, for Gannon, it was an afternoon of learning, his mentor a wily tutor. Tricks of the tracker's trade, so many of them to be stored in his memory. How to ascertain that scars on flat rock had been made by shod hooves. What to look out for when guiding his mount through brushy terrain or thick-grassed areas, indentations that were no longer indentations, but had been hours before. Study of leaves, of the bark of trees. The tell-tale marks indicating tracks had been obliterated by a blanket dragged by a tag rider. These and so many other dead giveaways.

He would, after all the advice offered by Smith, learn to rely not only on his eyes but on his sense of smell, his hearing.

'Get used to the maybes,' Smith stressed. 'You sight crows or quail, any kinda bird fly up sudden, maybe a coyote spooked 'em — or maybe they heard horses and you didn't.'

Gannon vowed to retain every hint in his memory, and hoped he could do that. Just before they parted, never to meet again, Smith pointed south to a series of rises.

'You'll likely sight their night fires 'tween now and when you find 'em. That'll mean they dunno you're bird-doggin'. But you don't have to stay frozen-assed. Safe enough for you to make a fire if you do like I told you. Big hill 'tween you and them. An overhang's right handy. Mind what I said about the right kinda wood. It burns slow, keeps you warm enough, but don't give off hardly no smoke.'

'And smother my fire before sun-up,' nodded Gannon. 'I'll remember, Jethro.' He offered his hand. 'And how do I begin thanking you?'

'You know how, so,' muttered Smith. 'Nail the sneakin' polecats — so they'll cause no more misery.'

Gannon resumed his hunt in better spirits, his optimism high.

★ ★ ★

At lunch in the dining car, Ella Cardew's curiosity again got the better of her. Max, Gerry and Hattie, the latter in particular, listened cautiously as she questioned Rick.

'Our encounter with those bank robbers, the way you turned the tables. I was scared out of my mind, but you seemed cool all the time — as if you knew exactly what to do and when to do it. You've been a law officer or a professional gunfighter or both, isn't that so?'

'Perish the thought,' shrugged Rick.

147

'I'd have no patience for the restrictions imposed on sheriffs and their deputies. They have to abide by certain rules of law. For instance, they can't pursue a runaway miscreant beyond the boundaries of the county they police. As for being a professional gunfighter . . . '

'You'd do fine, wouldn't you?' said Max. 'I mean — holy Moses — the way you handle a six-shooter . . . '

'Men who hire out their guns have a short life expectancy,' declared Rick. 'It was never my idea of a handy way to earn a dollar.'

'But it's almost as though you were ready for those outlaws,' argued Ella.

'I wasn't ready for them,' Rick assured her. 'In that kind of situation, all I can do is wait, hope for a distraction and take advantage of it.'

'You were relying on the Austrian?' challenged Ella, aiming a curt nod at Hattie. 'You *knew* she had that tiny pistol — in her *garter*?'

'*Himmel*!' exclaimed Hattie, and tried to blush.

'Take it easy, Ella,' chided Max.

'How *could* I know, Miss Cardew?' protested Rick.

'Dis is embarrassink,' mumbled Hattie.

'I didn't know about Inger's hide-away pistol,' lied Rick. 'But she's no stranger to me. I know her well enough to expect that, in time of danger, she keeps her nerve and — uh — thinks fast on her feet.'

'Well, she sure proved *that*,' recalled Max.

'I assumed Inger raised her skirts to draw attention away from me and give me my chance to start a counteraction,' said Rick. 'She certainly distracted those bandits.'

'*Molte grazie, signorina*!' grinned Geraldo, and rolled his eyes.

'The derringer was as much a surprise to me as to everybody else,' said Rick.

The star decided to believe that, but couldn't resist belittling Hattie. Her spite surfaced; she would never forget nor forgive a well-aimed kick to her shapely rear section.

'Only one way you could know about her garter pistol,' she sneered. 'I don't like you, Braddock, but I'm sure you're particular about women, and the kraut's certainly not your type.'

'Come on now, Ella,' winced Max. 'Inger doesn't deserve that.'

It was an awkward moment. Rick gagged on a half-chewed mouthful and did some worrying; just how much innuendo would his wife tolerate? Max frowned. Geraldo averted his eyes.

'Braddock does have style,' Ella persisted. 'But this Viennese frump?'

How would Hattie react? She kept her husband in suspense for only a moment. She was studying Ella, not angrily, not resentfully, but sadly.

'*Ich bin* . . . ' she began.

'How many times do I have to tell you?' snapped Ella. 'Use *English* when you speak to me.'

'I am sorry,' Hattie said gently.

'You got nothing to apologize for,

honey,' muttered Max.

'Nein, Herr Shelley,' murmured Hattie. 'Is not vot I mean.' She eyed Ella again. 'I am sorry for *you*, Madam. Ven a lady so *schon*, so beautiful, so famous, is so unkind, it means she is *nicht glucklich* — not a happy lady, *never* happy.' She shook her head dolefully. 'Is so sad.'

Ella turned pale and dropped her fork. She glared at Hattie as she came upright.

'Damn you!' she breathed. 'I don't need your sympathy!'

With that, she turned and left the dining car in high dudgeon, her meal unfinished. Max and Geraldo hastily gulped their coffee and rose to follow her. Rick was poker-faced, Hattie looking perplexed.

'Justa leave her to us,' mumbled Geraldo.

'Don't worry about this, honey,' soothed Max.

'I say something I shouldn't did?' frowned Hattie.

'Not your fault,' Max assured her. 'We'll take care of her. It's just — when Ella's steaming — it takes a little time for us to cool her down. She oughtn't be by herself at a time like this.'

Max and Geraldo made a fast exit from the dining car. The Braddocks continued their meal, quietly trading comments.

'You had a right, sweetheart,' muttered Rick. 'You've taken a lot from her, but there are limits.'

'I didn't overdo it?'

'She was out of line. It was a low blow. You wouldn't be you if you hadn't hit back.'

'Is she getting to us?' Hattie wondered. 'And are we overdoing the sympathy?'

'It's hard not to feel sorry for her,' Rick said pensively. 'Our attitude's normal enough, I believe. We can both remember times when we've seen some well-dressed citizen stumbling out of some Denver bar too drunk to know what he's doing. Sometimes it's funny. Other times it strikes us as pathetic.'

'Depending on our mood of the moment,' she supposed.

'What does it take to really reach a woman like her?' he wondered.

'A greater intelligence than yours or mine maybe, Rick. A psychologist with a streak of genius is one possibility. She's a case for treatment if I ever saw one.'

'Temperament I can understand. A lot of talented artists are as temperamental as Ella, but can be reasoned with. My problem — and yours — is we haven't found the key, haven't figured out *how* to reason with *her*. That was a clever comeback you gave her, honey. It really shook her.'

'That could be what she needs to bring her to her senses. A good shaking.'

Rick had finished eating. Hattie was pouring his coffee when he snapped his fingers, his eyes gleaming.

'Not shook,' he declared. 'The word is shock. There's a chance she could be shocked into going on the wagon, and *staying* on it.'

'How do we arrange that?' challenged Hattie. 'Confront her with a woman her own age, a long-time hard drinker looking raddled and ten years older?'

'Something like that,' he nodded. 'Something unexpected, right out of the blue, a hard jolt.'

'Gerry's a fine accompanist,' she reflected. 'It might help if he's also a convincing actor. Suppose, for instance, he pretended to take to the bottle, pretended to swig copiously of vino, made a hash of accompanying Ella, hit a few wrong notes half-way through her popular rendition of 'Drink To Me Only With Thine Eyes' and . . . ?'

'Whoah,' grinned Rick.

'What?' she demanded. 'Not strong enough?'

'It'd create the shock effect, but it'd be a dirty trick on Max,' he pointed out. 'He's got a lot riding on this tour. Bad publicity would be bad for business. The famous Geraldo Palestrina — her accompanist — drunk during a performance?'

'A little too drastic,' she conceded.

'Even if we dealt Max in on the plan, it'd be more than he could handle,' opined Rick. 'Ella's giving him trouble enough already, and let's not forget we like him.'

'The shock idea's still good,' she insisted.

'Right,' he agreed. 'One of our better ideas. But we'd best wait for the right time, the right place and the right opportunity.'

★ ★ ★

Late morning of this day, Barton Renshaw and three of his aides were playing the waiting game in a trappers' cabin an hour's ride north of Granger City. The absentee was Wes Trent, sent into the big town by Renshaw to check on the Cardew company's next venue and the area in proximity to it. Finding the shack and its pole corral deserted, Renshaw had reluctantly decided they should hole up here a while.

With its four sagging bunks and evil-smelling stove, this dismal hideaway was no place for a man as fastidious as the gang's leader; he sat on the edge of a rickety chair and refused to remove his duster. Joe Walston had investigated the stove and the fuel supply. He had broken out provisions and appointed himself cook. To Noad and Langland, Walston's efforts produced an appetizing aroma. To Renshaw, it was an odour. He was relieved when Langland, lounging in the open doorway as lookout, announced Trent was returning.

Staring southward to where the mountain trail wound south toward Granger City, Langland informed his cohorts,

'It's Wes. Just in time for lunch.'

'I'm delighted,' said Renshaw, grimacing. 'If he's acquired the necessary information, it will be my pleasure to depart this verminous hovel.'

Trent rode up, dismounted, off-saddled his horse and corraled it with the other animals. He then entered the cabin grinning his sardonic grin.

'Checked the whole layout, Bart,' he reported, seating himself at the rough table. 'Everything you wanted to know, I can show you.'

Renshaw consulted his newspaper again.

'They'll be playing a three-night engagement starting tomorrow night,' he said briskly. 'The venue is the Rialto Theatre. Accommodation provided by the Kingsley Hotel. How are those two places located?'

'On the main street, opposite each other,' said Trent. He fished out a pencil and spread a sheet of paper on the table. Renshaw watched intently as he began drawing a diagram. 'Here's the theatre. The street's fairly wide so, after the show, they have to cross it to here — the hotel. And, as in any other town of that size, you can bet they'll have an escort, local lawmen and probably extra deputies recruited for the occasion, to and from the theatre.'

'Were you able to inspect the register at the Kingsley Hotel?' demanded Renshaw.

'That part was easy,' said Trent, and pencilled some numbers. 'The lobby was crowded. The *town*'s crowded. I'd say the Cardew woman's manager hired himself a smart advance agent. Posters all over town, people arriving from all around to see her and not all of 'em wanting to camp outside the town limits. They were lining up at all the hotels, the boarding houses and even the cheap doss-houses. Well, the Kingsley lobby was jam-packed, so I did what every other jasper was doing, shouldered my way to the reception desk. The clerk was wide awake, but looked like he was having a nightmare.'

'Details,' ordered Renshaw. 'Don't ramble.'

'Okay, being sharp-eyed, and being close enough, I got these numbers,' said Trent. 'Four rooms have been reserved for the Cardew company. Upstairs rooms. She has one to herself, her manager and accompanist, Shelley and Palestrina, are sharing a double next door. She's in number twelve, they're in fourteen. Two singles right opposite, fifteen and seventeen. Her maid, Schmidt, will be in one of them. Some jasper name of Braddock's in the other.'

He was making another sketch. Renshaw studied it and urged him to print in the room numbers. As well as sneaking a look at the register, Trent had gone upstairs and taken note of the location of the rooms held for the star and her entourage.

'You've indicated a room at the end of the corridor with an 'X',' Renshaw observed. 'Kindly explain.'

'Bathroom,' said Trent. 'It's a handsome hotel, Bart. Probably the finest in Granger City. Nothing but the best for the famous Ella Cardew. But it's old. Suites don't include bathrooms.

And that one bathroom's reserved for the Carew outfit. There was a sign fixed to the door.'

'It's a rear room?' asked Renshaw. Trent nodded. 'And there's a street behind the hotel?'

'Kind of narrow,' Trent told him. 'More a back alley than a back street.'

'Residential?'

'Sure. I took a look.'

'Miss Cardew may give only one performance in Granger City.' When Renshaw said that, Trent and the other men eyed him expectantly. He showed them a bland smile and remarked, 'The unexpected, and the totally unsuspected, always confounds lawmen. They're never prepared to cope with audacity, so they're more inclined to believe the obvious.'

Walston and Noad traded puzzled frowns.

'Bart,' said Langland. 'You want to make that a little clearer?'

'After we leave for Granger City, I'll be studying the surrounding terrain as I always do,' said Renshaw. 'After we reach our destination, I'll acquaint myself with the region close to the Kingsley Hotel. And it's possible, gentlemen, that on *this* occasion we may be spared the necessity to remove our hostage to some pre-chosen hiding place far from town. She may be kept closer at hand — which is the last thing her manager or the local law officers would suspect. Indeed, the possibility would *never* occur to them.'

Trent whistled softly. Walston winced and complained,

'Sounds risky.'

Renshaw's reaction unnerved him.

'I do not take risks, Walston!' The boss-kidnapper was glaring at him. 'Fools take risks! Brilliant strategists rely on audacity! Would you dare to call me . . . ?'

'Hey, I'd never call you a fool,' Walston hastened to assure him. 'None of us would. You know that.'

Regaining his composure, Renshaw said testily,

'I suppose we've no choice but to eat whatever you've been cooking. We'll then resume our journey to Granger City.'

'Same routine,' Langland assumed.

'We ride in at intervals, separately and from different directions,' nodded Renshaw. He looked at Trent again. 'You did remember to scout for a suitable rendezvous?'

'A saloon called the Brass Rail on Alvarado Road,' said Trent. 'I looked it over. There are back rooms for private poker parties, kind of rooms we've used before. Safe enough. If we keep our voices down, we could be laying plans to rob every bank in town and it wouldn't matter, nobody'd hear.'

'You may serve our meal,' Renshaw ordered Walston. 'Then we'll be on our way. I am most eager to appraise prospects in Granger City.'

6

For sale or Rent

It was 2.10 pm when the southbound riders sighted the big town. Renshaw then gave the order for his companions to separate. Then he rode on alone, his mind busy again.

Big though it was, no doubt boasting many hotels and boarding houses, Granger City would be filling up, he realized. By tomorrow, when the great star arrived to play her three-night engagement at the Rialto Theatre, the town would be tight-packed, accommodation at a premium. Amazing — he chuckled to himself — amazing what could be achieved in a crowded town, if carefully planned.

A short time later he was riding unhurriedly into a main thoroughfare bordered by stores, saloons, hotels and other more imposing edifices, evidence of Granger City's growing prosperity. There were places of business on the many side streets angling east and west from the main stem, also the town's residential areas.

He had to visit several livery stables and resort to bribery in order to reserve stalls for his and his cohorts' horses. After that, he found hitching space for his mount a half-block from the area in which he was most interested.

The garish facade of the Rialto Theatre warranted only a cursory appraisal. He joined the queue at the ticket window and succeeded in purchasing seats for the first performance; singles in various parts of the theatre were more readily available than double or group reservations.

From the theatre, he crossed the broad street to enter the lobby of the Kingsley Hotel. It was as crowded as when his spy had checked the register, people clamouring at the two harassed men behind the reception counter, the desk clerk and the hotel manager, the latter running out of patience. The staircase was busy, guests ascending or coming down from their rooms, so the nondescript stranger climbing to the upper floor went unnoticed.

Renshaw checked the location of the reserved rooms noted by Wes Trent, returned to the lobby, made his exit and moved along to the side alley to saunter to the rear of the hotel. The back street, as Trent had said, was no wider than most back alleys.

He walked south, passed the rear of a two-storey residence, then paused to study the next building along, a ramshackle place with no upper storey and its back windows boarded up. An idea was growing in his mind as he glanced back to the hotel. Firestairs led up to its rear upper gallery, he observed. He liked the idea and smugly toyed with it, letting it develop. Audacity. The unpredictable. Those were its best features.

The vacant house's rear door opened

onto the alley's east side. To inspect its frontage, he made his way to the street running parallel with Main. And saw what he hoped to see. The front windows also boarded up, a sign fixed to the front fence announcing these premises to be 'For Sale Or Rent. Agents, Selwood & Son, Vigram Road.'

Locating the estate agent's office was no problem; a passer-by offered directions. He entered briskly, his air of authority giving the lie to his general appearance. Raymond Selwood Senior was alone in the office, a skinny, bespectacled, effusive individual, the archetypal real estate agent of those times. He greeted his caller with a bland smile and invited him to be seated. Renshaw did so and quietly informed him,

'I wish to enquire about the house two doors south of the Kingsley Hotel. The sign reads For Sale Or Rent.'

'That old place?' Selwood was taken aback. 'We never expected to find anther tenant for it, certainly not a

166

buyer. As a matter of fact, we've decided to have it demolished. It's our intention to build a better home on that site.'

'But it's still for rent?'

'Well, yes. And it's furnished. But I'm afraid the inside is in as poor condition as — uh — as much of the property as you've inspected. You'll have observed it's a frame structure and quite old.'

'I will require it for only a short time, a week at most.'

'You — actually wish to rent it, Mister . . . ?'

'My card,' said Renshaw. He produced his wallet. It contained, as well as money, several calling cards acquired from a job printer who never asked questions. The two banknotes he tossed onto the blotter won Selwood's eager attention. Next, he chose a card. Before proffering it, he warned softly, compellingly, 'From this moment on, our business is strictly private and confidential. You will discuss it with nobody, not even your son. Is that understood?'

'You may rely on my discretion,' Selwood assured him. He accepted the card and blinked at it. The inscription was impressive. 'D. W. Ridley, Special Investigator, Pinkerton Detective Agency.' His eyebrows shot up. '*Well*, sir — Mister Ridley — you may most *certainly* rely on my discretion.'

'Consider yourself sworn to secrecy,' Renshaw said grimly, and snapped his fingers. 'The card, if you please.'

'Yes, Mister Ridley.'

Selwood returned the card. Renshaw carefully slid it back into position, pocketed his wallet and nodded to the cash on the blotter. 'Make out a receipt for that.'

'At once, sir, but this is far more than . . . '

'The entire amount, Mister Selwood. In time of crisis, the agency does not pinch pennies.'

'Most generous.'

'For the extra, you will guarantee me

maximum co-operation and complete secrecy.' Renshaw leaned forward in his chair, fixed the estate agent with his eyes and delivered his spiel. 'The matter being dealt with by me and my four associates is of vital importance to the government, also extremely delicate. For four days, perhaps the whole week, we'll be engaged in important discussions of our assignment. We'll also be planning strategy. That's all you need to know, Mister Selwood. I'm working with fellow-operatives of my choice and, as we're unconcerned with creature comforts, that house will be ideal for our purpose.'

'Of — national importance?' whispered Selwood.

'So much so,' declared Renshaw, 'that you are now duty-bound to protect our secret.'

'When do you — uh — wish to take up residence . . . ?'

'It's better you don't know. And safer for you.'

'S-s-safer?'

'No more questions, Mister Selwood.'

'Depend on me, sir. My lips are sealed.'

'It won't be necessary for the boards to be removed from the windows, but the sign must go. Much of our planning will continue into the night, and lamplight in a supposedly unoccupied dwelling is apt to arouse curiosity.'

'I'll see to it at once.'

'Do so. And now, if you please, the receipt — and the keys. How many?'

'Just the two. Front and back doors.'

When he returned to Main Street, the boss-kidnapper was his usual inscrutable self, but inwardly complimenting himself. He anticipated his aides would suffer a shock reaction when he outlined his plan. Well, that was typical of them. They were reliable enough and he needed them but, in the final analysis, they were his hangers-on, his to command.

He spent some time scouting the area dominated by the theatre and the

Kingsley Hotel and satisfying himself that Granger County's seat of law and order, the office of Sheriff A. J. Barclay fronting the county jail, was located a full four blocks away.

When he finally found his way to Alvarado Road and moved into the Brass Rail Saloon, he was beckoned by the hefty man lounging in the open doorway of a back room, Joe Walston. The others had arrived and were waiting for him. He crossed the barroom and traded nods with Walston.

Trent, Noad and Langland were seated at a card table. There was a bottle of bourbon as yet uncorked. The bottle, the five glasses, ashtrays and a new deck completed the desired effect; a private poker party. Walston followed Renshaw in, closing the door behind him.

Renshaw chose a chair and got down to business, beginning by listing the names of the livery stables at which accommodation had been reserved for their horses.

'As for our accommodation . . . ' He smiled complacently and told of his arrangement with the real estate agency. 'The place is rundown of course, but its proximity to the hotel is important to my strategy. I've decided Miss Cardew will be removed from that upstairs bathroom or her bedroom, whichever she happens to be occupying, and transferred to the house by way of that back street. The usual note will be left, this time addressed to her manager, Shelley.' While his aides listened in stunned silence, he continued. 'The note will ensure there'll be no hue and cry, everything handled quietly as usual. But we depart from previous procedure. Instead of keeping our hostage in some remote corner of the county, she'll be kept right there in the house with us — close to where she was seized — the last place a search party would expect to find her. Not that there'll be a search party.'

He paused to calmly study the faces of four murderous rogues who, judging by their expressions, feared their ears were deceiving them. There was a suggestion of desperation in the way Noad uncorked the bottle and half-filled the five glasses. All but Renshaw swigged quickly. First to speak, Langland, the big redhead, could only manage an exclamation.

'Hell's bells!'

Trent fumbled to light a cigar, eyed Renshaw warily and muttered,

'That's close, Bart. You're the boss. I don't argue. I'm just asking — isn't this — you know — pushing our luck?'

'Luck has nothing to do with it,' said Renshaw. 'In other respects, such as collection of the ransom, we'll be adhering to our foolproof system. Shelley, travelling alone, will make the delivery. The ideal place would be a quiet area just this side of the county line. We'll be waiting for him at the pre-arranged time — all of us. He won't have to look for us. It's only necessary for one man to meet him. The pay-off will be tallied. He'll then be told where to find the hostage and, by the time he returns to town to rescue his star from that dump, we'll be out of Granger Country and well on our way to New Mexico — with no descriptions circulating.'

'If some citizen gets curious . . . ' began Trent.

'The agent from whom I've rented the property believes we're Pinkertons,' Renshaw reminded him. 'To him, this is an adventure, probably the most exciting experience of his humdrum life. We can depend on him to ensure our privacy.'

'What it means,' Walston said uneasily, 'is the Cardew woman'll have to be kept gagged, hog-tied and blindfolded all the time we're holding her. That means we can't feed her. We loosen her gag, she's apt to holler. So how long . . . ?'

'I estimate it should take her manager less than four days to arrange delivery of the cash from San Francisco to here,' said Renshaw. 'Calm yourself. No reason she should starve. Confronted by one hooded man preparing to spoon-feed her and another holding a knife to her face, threatening to disfigure her if she dares make a sound, I doubt she'll scream.'

'You're thinking of everything, as usual,' grinned Noad.

'And reconsidering my original notion,' said Renshaw. 'I've decided we should take her after her final performance, not her first night.'

'That'd be a whole lot better,' nodded Langland. 'Too much commotion if she disappears after her first show. The local law would buy in even if Shelley didn't tip 'em off.'

'I'm delighted you agree.' Renshaw smiled his prim smile. 'The company's extended stay in Granger City will easily be explained. Shelley will think of a reason everybody will believe. Exhausted after three consecutive performances to packed houses, the lady is resting, confined to her bed and receiving no visitors — during which time her manager will be keeping busy.'

'She's in for a big welcome here,' remarked Trent. 'I guess you've all noticed placards everywhere. Not just around the theatre. All over town.'

'An hour from now,' Renshaw said after consulting his watch, 'we'll move into the old house.'

* * *

The southbound made a brief stop in Pedroza during the run to Granger City. A bundle of newspapers was tossed to the conductor. Passengers stayed aboard, but Pedroza folk lined both sides of the railroad tracks, staring at the Pullman cars in hopes of catching a glimpse of the famous soprano. Urged on by her manager, Ella reluctantly emerged onto an observation platform with him to acknowledge her noisy admirers; she offered a sweet smile and waved graciously.

When the train rolled again, Max and Geraldo joined Ella in her private compartment. Discussion of her repertoire began; the programmes of her three Granger City performances had to be planned. It was down to business for the star, her manager and accompanist, so her protectors were able to share a seat and catch up on talk again.

'She's being as tricky as ever,' confided Hattie. 'Must be some kind of genius when it comes to secreting the hard stuff.'

'Keeping you busy?' asked Rick.

A steward moved along the passage, delivering newspapers. Rick accepted one, folded it on his lap and gave Hattie his ear.

'I had to confiscate a bottle of perfume,' she complained. 'The label had me fooled at first. 'Parfum de Extase', but, oh husband mine, when I pulled the stopper and took a sniff . . . '

'Cognac?'

'That parfum was of Kentucky, not

177

La Belle France. Good old aged-in-the-wood sourmash whiskey. I thought she'd go for my jugular when I tossed it out the window.'

'I'd toss *her* out of a window if she ever harmed you. I try to be as gallant a bodyguard as possible, but *you're* the one who arouses my protective instincts more than any other female of the species.'

'My loyal and possessive husband, ever-ready to leap to my defence.'

'Must be exciting for you,' he suggested.

'Never a dull moment,' she chuckled, then nodded to the paper. 'Any reviews of the tour?'

'If there are, they're bound to be favourable,' he predicted. He opened the paper. Together, they scanned the front page. Leafing his way to Page 5, he found a glowing report of the Denver, Steeple Rock and Ibanez engagements. They traded a comment or two, after which he turned back to Page 2. There, a two-column story caught his eye and, suddenly oblivious to his wife, he read every word of it. 'Oh, hell!'

'What is it, darling? Don't tell me there's been a fire in Denver — at the barber shop? I love that apartment of ours.'

'Something more serious, to put it mildly.' He startled Hattie by aiming a scowl at the closed door of the star's private compartment. 'I'm working the wrong assignment. Keeping Ella dry doesn't matter a damn — not compared to *this* case!'

'Cool down, dear,' she frowned. 'Don't give it to me to read. Just summarize it for me.'

'They've been at it so long, and they're still at large, no clues to their identity, no descriptions,' he said bitterly. He offered her a terse account of all he had read of the homicidal kidnappers now referred to by frontier newsmen as The Five Deadly Shadows, their depredations, the brutal killings, the bankroll they were building, cash, ransom paid by kin of their stealthily seized hostages, and the fact that they were operating over a wide area; no guessing where they would strike next. 'Think about it, honey. They make it so *easy* for themselves . . . '

'It's tragic and I'm as disgusted as you,' she murmured. 'But don't brood about it, don't let this get to you. We have our hands full and we can't afford distraction. They can't *stay* at large. Don't underestimate county sheriffs and the Federal marshals. Those lowdowns will be apprehended.'

'You forgot to add eventually,' he retorted. 'Hattie, I don't underestimate lawmen of any kind, nor do I doubt they're trying to investigate and doing the best they can, but what've they got? Nothing. No leads, no clues. We're talking about five anonymous men who leave nothing to chance, who kill their back-trail, who've never shown their faces. It's like hunting phantoms.'

Hattie sighed and shook her head.

'Altruism is most commendable, but

you're overdoing it, my dear,' she softly warned. 'Don't let this become an obsession. You're a brilliant investigator in your own way, but you can't fight every law-breaker in the West.'

'Sure,' he agreed. 'Just let me stew in my own frustration a while.'

'Only natural you feel anger.'

'Fury's the word. It infuriates me that it's all so simple for them. Nobody can identify them and they choose their victims with care. Chances are they travel separately. Without their hoods and dusters, they probably look harmless, not the kind to arouse a lawman's suspicion. They could be rigged as out-of-work cowhands or farmhands. They're the most dangerous trash I've read about in a long time but, if I met any of them face to face, would I be leery of them? It's more likely I'd assume them to be quite pleasant jaspers. Butter wouldn't melt in their mouths.'

'Sobering thought, darling. As actors — playing the roles that suit their purpose — they could be as convincing as we are?'

'I wish you hadn't said that,' complained Rick, wincing.

'Sorry,' she shrugged.

'Too late,' he grouched. 'You said it. And you could be right.'

'Is it out of your system now?'

'Uh huh. No more brooding. Back to normal.'

'That means back to our assignment. And, so far, so good. We oughtn't be complacent, but . . .'

'Sure. We're earning what Max's paying us. Tricky Ella's been sober since Denver. She's not enjoying it, but it's better for her health and Max's nerves.'

'You know, she really is intelligent,' frowned Hattie. 'So I'm surprised that, by now, she hasn't lost her craving for firewater.'

'I'm still a little confused about that,' said Rick. 'But I think I'll stick with my first hunch. She needs this tour, but hates the travelling, and she's too mule-stubborn to acknowledge that Max set it up for the good of her career.'

'A waning career,' offered Hattie, 'according to a remark or two I've overheard.'

'So Max has become her whipping boy,' he decided. 'Instead of appreciating what he's trying to achieve for her, she decided to resent it. And this is her way of punishing him. He sweats when she tries to sneak a bottle past him.'

'That's spite.' Hattie grimaced in disapproval. 'She *is* intelligent, but not a nice person.'

'Meanwhile, we make Granger City noon tomorrow,' he said. 'Another big welcome for Ella and a sell-out three-night engagement.'

'With the Braddock Detective Agency on the job every minute,' she smiled.

★ ★ ★

His cohorts knew him to be fastidious to a fault, but Renshaw seemed more than satisfied with their temporary quarters. The old house so conveniently close to the rear of the Kingsley Hotel needed dusting and cleaning — a lot of dusting and cleaning — but he insisted it was ideal for their needs and the last place in Granger County a lawman would suspect the hostage to be held captive, even if Max Shelley were fool enough to report her disappearance.

While Walston and the others set about making the place as livable as possible, Renshaw chose a room for himself. It opened off the right side of the corridor running from the inner kitchen doorway to the door opening onto the street paralleling Main. Suitable to his needs, he assured himself. A bed, a table, a chair. He was prepared to rough it. The hostage bound, gagged and blindfolded, was welcome to the bed. All hers, after her closing show at the Rialto.

He had pen and ink, but required paper and an envelope. Walston was assigned to purloin these necessities from the lobby of some downtown hotel. And for Horrie Langland he had a special chore.

'While daylight is holding, you'll ride west to the county border. Use the regular trail and keep a sharp eye out for concealment from whence Shelley can be sighted when he fetches the ransom money. And remember — concealment for all five of us. Usual procedure. One of us will meet him, collect the cash and tell him where to find his meal ticket. After he heads back to town, we depart from Granger County.'

The heavyset redhead grinned mirthlessly.

'Let it be me meets him, Bart. I want to see the look on his face when I tell him where she's stashed.'

'I'll keep you in mind,' said Renshaw. 'Get along now.' Langland hurried out. Wes Trent then answered his summons. 'Take these tickets. Go to the theatre and exchange them. They're for the first show. Now that I've changed my plan, we'll need tickets for the last performance. Anywhere in the house, five singles, understood?'

'Good as done,' Trent assured him on his way out.

While fixing coffee in the dilapidated kitchen, Waldo Noad muttered a reminder.

'Once she's in our hands, we'll have to tight-guard this dump. How do you want us to handle it?'

'One man outside that rear door,' said Renshaw. 'Two just inside the front door. Both entrances will be kept locked. You and the others will take turn at guard duty. The woman will be kept in my room.' He thought again of the estate agent and mentally congratulated himself. 'It's unlikely we'll be bothered by intruders — most unlikely. But, as always, we'll take every precaution.'

Later, when Walston returned with the stationery, Renshaw retired to his room to pen the ransom demand. He first tore the top inch, the hotel letterhead, from a sheet. Then he inked his pen and began printing.

'SHELLEY,

SAFE RETURN OF OUR HOSTAGE IS GUARANTEED UPON PAYMENT OF THE SUM OF $100,000. YOU WILL IMMEDIATELY ARRANGE SHIPMENT OF THAT AMOUNT — IN CASH — BY YOUR WEST COAST CONTACTS OR THROUGH A LOCAL BANK.

BE WARNED THAT THE DISAPPEARANCE IS TO BE KEPT SECRET. YOU WILL LET IT BE KNOWN MISS CARDEW IS CONFINED TO HER ROOM. DO *NOT* ADVISE THE LAW AUTHORITIES. YOU WILL BE WATCHED AND, IF THERE IS ANY ATTEMPT AT A SEARCH, IF WE HAVE THE SLIGHTEST SUSPICION THESE INSTRUCTIONS ARE BEING DISOBEYED, YOU WILL NEVER SEE THE LADY AGAIN. SHE WILL BE DISPOSED OF AND IT IS UNLIKELY HER BODY WILL EVER BE FOUND.

YOU WILL RECEIVE FURTHER INSTRUC-TIONS WHEN THE MONEY IS IN YOUR POSSESSION.'

He folded the sheet, sealed it in

the envelope and printed the name 'M. Shelley.'

When Trent returned to the house, he handed Renshaw five tickets for the third and final performance.

'For a couple of us, it'll be standing room only, but what the hell?' he shrugged. 'What's important is we'll all get a good clear look at her.' He then offered a suggestion. 'How do you like this idea, Bart? Whoever grabs her has to carry her from her bedroom, the bathroom or whatever and back here through the rear door. And, in case he's spotted, nobody better see what he's carrying.'

'Obviously,' nodded Renshaw.

'Grain sack,' grinned Walston. 'Nothing to it. A fist in the right place'll put her to sleep. Then you pull the sack over her and . . . '

'This'll be better than a grain sack, Bart,' declared Trent. 'There's a laundry uptown a little way, big place doing big business. And get this. They supply sacks to their regular customers.

Name of the place in big print. Davis Laundry. Easy enough for one of us to get hold of one of those sacks. So, if anybody who ought to be home in bed sees a couple men headed here — toting that kind of sack . . . '

'I approve,' said Renshaw. 'A familiar sight to the locals, somebody carrying a bagful of laundry. I commend you, Wes. You're learning.'

'So we're all set,' enthused Noad.

'We need only wait for the much-admired Miss Cardew and her people,' said Renshaw. 'And her final performance here.'

It was after sundown when Langland rejoined them. He was in time for the indifferent supper cooked by Trent. Hungry though he was, he reported to Renshaw before settling down to eat.

'It's not too long a ride, Bart. You'll approve the layout. You wanted rocks to hide us, you got 'em, big ones, a whole cluster of 'em about thirty yards from the sign marking the county border. Safe set-up. We'll see Shelley coming when he's a mile away.'

'Very satisfactory,' decided Renshaw.

During the meal, Noad asked,

'Want to be there, Bart? The depot, when the showfolks arrive. Be quite a sight to see, probably the whole town turning out to give the singing woman a big welcome.'

'We'll view the scene from a distance,' Renshaw said testily. 'Crowds irritate me. I intensely dislike being jostled.'

★ ★ ★

Late afternoon of this day, Noah Gannon was seeking a suitable site for a nightcamp. The waterhole he approached appeared just right. There was feed grass for his horse, and the area was not too far from the tracks he had been following, tracks he might never have detected but for the comprehensive tutoring of Jethro Smith.

He had almost reached the waterhole when the plodding hoofbeats, a jingle of harness and the metallic clattering sounds warned him some kind of vehicle was headed northward along the trail.

Turning in his saddle, he studied the oncoming rig and decided its driver would cause him no problems. An itinerant pedlar for sure. The bright colours of the printing adorning the canvas of the wagon drawn by a couple of broad-backed bays left him in no doubt. From his perch, the cigar-puffing driver waved in friendly fashion, gestured to the waterhole and called to him.

'Camping space enough for both of us! You mind some company?'

'It's free country,' replied Gannon. 'Come ahead.'

He was seeing to the comfort of his horse when the pedlar arrived, stalled his team and climbed down to unhitch them.

'Christie's the name, Abe, if you want to be friendly.' He grinned affably, a tubby, cheery character whose checkered suit and beaver hat had seen better days. 'And you don't win a prize for guessing the business I'm in.'

'Noah Gannon.' He responded to Christie's greeting with a preoccupied nod. 'Sure. The way your stock rattles, you'd have to be a general storekeeper on wheels. A little of everything?'

'Drygoods, ladies' geegaws, pots and pans, potions for anything that ails you,' bragged Christie. 'You name it, I hawk it.'

'I'm running low on provisions but, between us, maybe we have enough for a passable supper,' suggested Gannon.

'We won't starve,' Christie assured him.

'Fine,' said Gannon. 'While you're tending your team, I'll hunt up some firewood.'

Later, when they were squatting by their fire and accounting for a thrown-together but adequate meal, he asked only one question. Like all of his kind, Christie had the gift of the gab. He heard and answered the question in the negative — had he sighted five riders southbound? — and resumed his description of the big town he had passed through the day before.

'Didn't make any sales in Granger City. I was just passing through, you understand. In my business, you find a big town like Granger, you don't try to drum up any trade. Local merchants don't approve, so neither does the local law. It's in out-of-the way settlements, little places, I find customers who'll buy my wares.'

Gannon was well aware of this, but didn't say as much, just kept on chewing and listening. Thus he learned, as his informant had, of the air of expectancy in Granger City, all the excitement following Billy Beale's deal with the owner of the Rialto Theatre and the tacking of posters all over town. The famous Ella Cardew was on her way, scheduled for a three-nights engagement.

'But I was tempted to stay on, Noah,

maybe buy a ticket. Well, she'd be a sight for sore eyes, no question about that, supposed to be a mighty beautiful woman, but I'd be wasting my money. You see, I have this defect. Don't worry, you can't catch it from me. Ever meet a tone-deaf man before?'

'Can't say I have.'

'Mind now, I don't complain. It's my only defect that I know of and it doesn't bother me a whole lot. It's just, when I hear music or somebody singing, it doesn't mean anything to me. I wouldn't even recognize the tune. If they're off key, I wouldn't know it.'

'A man doesn't miss what he never had?'

'Exactly how I feel about it, Noah.'

The pedlar held forth on the accommodation crisis in Granger City, every hotel, boarding house, even the lowliest hole-in-the-wall places filled to capacity, as would be the Rialto for all three performances by the famous star.

Later, bedding down by the fire while Christie bunked in his wagon, Gannon wondered about the kidnappers. Would they pull off another coup in Granger City? The possibility could not be ignored. Pickpockets, panhandlers, every kind of sneakthief plied their shabby trade in crowded towns. It might be that, if his quarry planned on seizing a member of some wealthy family of Granger City, this could be the ideal time, local lawmen preoccupied with protection of a popular performer. He had a vague memory of reading of her admirers running riot in towns played during this tour.

It was a real possibility. He should, he assured himself, visit Granger City. But he felt frustrated, well realizing that, if sighted and remembered by any of five men *he* wouldn't recognize, he could be signing his own death warrant. He would be seen as a threat. Once seen and identified, his doom would be sealed. All right, why play into their hands?

'It doesn't have to be broad daylight,' he decided before sleep claimed him. 'When I start checking around, it'll be long after sundown, and I'll be moving clear of the bright lights.'

7

Woman Missing

It was to be the biggest welcome accorded the troupe since the arrival in Denver.

By 11.50 of that memorable morning, the sidewalks of Granger City's main street were thronged. Locals had turned out in their Sunday-best; it might have been 4th of July. The mayor had organized the local brass band and now the musicians were tuning up at the railroad depot. A special dais had been erected. Townfolk supposed this was inevitable. Their mayor and other dignitaries would deliver speeches of welcome, but nobody minded; word had spread that the speakers intended keeping it short, no prolonged orations. Wagons were in position, their drivers ready to load the showfolks' baggage and transport it to the Kingsley Hotel. For transportation of the star and her retinue, two surreys had been provided.

Well to the fore and in good humour was Gus White, owner of the Rialto Theatre, well-groomed, nearing middle age, of pleasing appearance and nobody's fool. Of all the citizens of Granger County, White understood showfolk best. Before leaving town, leaving placards all over Granger City, Billy Beale had sworn White to secrecy and taken him into his confidence regarding Ella Cardew's 'little weakness'. This had not shaken White's poise. Ella's bodyguards were to learn that, in Augustus White, veteran showman, they had a shrewd, sharp-eyed ally.

Keeping busy, staying alert, were the burly A. J. Barclay, sheriff of Granger County, his regular deputies and four special deputies recruited for this great occasion. Young bloods apt to act rashly at first sight of the beautiful Ella had been duly warned; several cells of the county jail were reserved for any fools attempting to take liberties.

Aboard the train, with their destination almost in sight, Max Shelley delivered last minute instructions to his people, crowded into the compartment he shared with Geraldo.

'You're a pro, Ella, so you know what to expect and how to handle it. No need for you to make a speech. Same old routine. I'll respond to the speeches of welcome on your behalf, remind everybody your voice is your fortune and you have to save it for your performance.'

'As if I'd have anything to say to these frontier rubes,' she retorted disdainfully.

Max continued,

'Gerry, I estimate you'll be testing the theatre piano within ninety minutes of our arrival. That'll give you all the time you need, *if* it needs a little tuning. Probably won't. Billy's last wire assures us Gus White runs a high-class business. Rick and Inger, you don't need any instructions at all.'

'We'll know what to do, and be ready to do it if we have to,' shrugged Rick.

'*Ja, Herr* Shelley,' nodded Hattie.

'Even her eagerness irritates me,' complained Ella. 'I swear, when this tour ends and I'm rid of her, I'll never eat strudel again.'

'Or drink schnapps, Madam?' smiled Hattie.

'Insolent bitch!' gasped Ella.

'Lady, will you never let up?' chided Rick. While she gaped at him, while Max and Geraldo flinched, he said his piece quietly, but vehemently. 'Whatever became of your sense of humour? The girl's not goading you. You can't take a joke? Don't interrupt. Just listen.'

'Uh — Rick . . . ' began Max.

'This has to be said,' declared Rick. 'Try to understand this, Ella. We're being well paid, but we're no longer working this assignment just for the money. You're a hard woman to like, but we do like you, we admire you a lot, we *care* about you.' He turned to Hattie. 'Am I speaking for you?'

'Ooh, ja, Herr Braddock,' Hattie nodded emphatically.

'So chew on that thought, Ella,' advised Rick. 'You're a smart woman with a lot of style — so *act* smart. A wise woman never resents people devoted to her welfare.'

Ella found her voice. Glaring at Max, she demanded,

'Are you going to just stand there and let him talk to me that way?'

Max shrugged helplessly and replied, 'I'd look stupid trying to gag Rick. And, besides, he speaks for all four of us, Ella. If Gerry and me tried to explain our feelings for you, you'd call us a couple of sentimental fools. And that's the truth.'

Rick cocked an ear. The train was slowing and the brass band already performing.

'Big reception coming up,' he said briskly. 'Everybody ready?'

'Knock 'em dead, Ella honey,' urged

Max. 'The big smile, the friendly wave — that's all it takes.'

Noisy though it was, the big welcome proceeded smoothly. After the south-bound steamed to a halt, Ella descended from the Pullman arm in arm with her manager and with Geraldo and the Braddocks following. The cheering was a threat to the mastoids. Max and his star were conducted onto the dais by the mayor, two councilmen, the sheriff and the urbane Gus White.

At the mayor's signal, the drummer clashed his cymbals and the brass stopped blaring. The speeches were mercifully short, not that the townfolk listened; smiling Ella had them hypnotized. Max spoke on her behalf, winning the crowd with a shameless lie, declaring that, since this tour began, his star had counted the days, all the time yearning to visit this fine town. The people were ecstatic, the applause thunderous; Rick half expected they'd start throwing money.

The troupe's progress from the depot

to the Kingsley Hotel was orderly, thanks to close surveillance by the local lawmen.

It was during lunch that Gus White managed a few words in private with Max, assured him he'd been alerted by Billy Beale and promised discretion. Not only Ella's bodyguard and dresser would be warding off bearers of liquid gifts; the stagehands at the Rialto could be relied upon to co-operate.

'Thought I'd tip you on the quiet, Max. For the sake of your blood pressure?'

'Gus, you're a real gent. Thanks a lot.'

During the afternoon, while the star rested under Hattie's watchful eye, while Max allowed himself a much-needed catnap, while Geraldo proved the piano at the Rialto was perfectly tuned by entertaining the backstage bunch, Rick made himself comfortable in the hotel's sumptuously furnished lobby, seating himself in earshot of the reception desk and perusing the current edition of the local newspaper.

It didn't surprise him that Ella was being given the front page treatment with the list of her successes spilling over onto Page 2. But then he became absorbed in another report, a rehash of the abductions and murders perpetrated by five marauders still eluding the law. He was brooding again, until a dapper local presented himself at the reception desk and addressed the clerk on duty. He carried a bouquet and a wrapped bottle. Rick fixed a jaundiced eye on him.

' 'Afternoon, Mister Fordice,' the clerk greeted him politely, but warily.

'My card, Vince,' grinned the visitor. 'You know what I'm here for. Take it up to Miss Cardew and tell her Granger City's foremost photographer's paying a courtesy call.'

'Sorry,' said the clerk. 'Miss Cardew's resting. No visitors. I have my orders.'

'She'll see me,' Fordice said confidently. 'She's a star, Vince. This is what they expect. Flowers. And the bottle? Not soda pop, not sarsasparilla. Imported champagne, Vince. The best — and it cost me.'

'Can't be done,' insisted the clerk.

'Sure, Vince, I can take a hint,' said Fordice, and produced a $10 bill. 'All yours. And another of the same when I leave.'

The clerk ignored the banknote and suggested right now would be the best time for him to leave.

'That's good advice,' said Rick, rising and approaching the desk.

'I don't know you,' frowned Fordice.

'The name's Braddock,' Rick informed him. 'Private detective hired to protect Miss Cardew.'

'Hey, I'm an admirer,' protested Fordice. 'The lady doesn't need protection against gentlemen callers, respectable businessmen.'

'I could have you arrested for this,' growled Rick. 'Talking about the champagne, feller. Exhaustive scientific tests prove conclusively that, when consumed by professional singers, especially sopranos, champagne adversely affects the larynx. Worse than that . . . '

'What?' blinked Fordice.

' . . . the acidic content of champagne is known to cause bombosis of the vocal cords,' continued Rick. 'A few sips at the wrong time can inflict carbuncular tonsilitis, if not a disastrous abdominal combustion.' He added sternly, 'Article seventy-five, Section thirteen of the Crimes Act of California — which I've no doubt is in force in this state also — states that the presentation of champagne to professional singers must be regarded as being as serious as attempted poisoning.'

'Lord Almighty!' gasped the photographer.

Rick consulted his watch.

'I'm gonna give you a break,' he said. 'I should send for the sheriff but, if you're out of here by the time I count to three . . . '

'I'm going, I'm going,' mumbled Fordice, and tossed the bouquet onto the desk. 'For your wife, Vince. Forget

I was here — please?'

Rick didn't have to begin counting. He and the clerk suddenly had the lobby to themselves. The clerk challenged with a wry grin,

'Bombosis? Abdominal combustion?'

'In my business, we learn to improvise,' shrugged Rick.

'Very effective,' remarked the clerk. 'And we're very discreet here at the Kingsley. Seems Gus White had a few words with the boss. The whole staff's been alerted. I'm sorry for Miss Cardew but, if she tries to wheedle any of us into slipping her a little of the hard stuff, she's in for a big disappointment.'

'Which won't improve her disposition,' said Rick. 'Well, Vince, that's life.'

★ ★ ★

The opening night of the star's Granger City engagement was a resounding success. Being a professional, Ella kept the lid on her frustration and

207

her compulsion to outwit Max, at least while on stage and captivating a capacity audience. Granger City folk loved her. Had they but realized it, their prolonged applause of every song cut two other ballads from the programme.

And so her closing number, calling for no great exertion of her impressive soprano, was a lilting rendition of *Believe Me If All Those Endearing Young Charms* performed centre stage to Geraldo's reverent accompaniment. No gestures. She stood in the spotlight with hands clasped, offering it with feeling, perfect enunciation of every word of the lyric. In the audience, some women dabbed at their eyes; many a male citizen had a lump in his throat.

Watching from the wings, Hattie whispered to Rick,

'You know, my dear, despite her overdone artistic temperament and her hellcat disposition, she's quite a psychologist. Her choice of a song for closing the show was brilliant.'

'That sentimental old chestnut,' nodded Rick. 'The effect couldn't be more dynamic if she were singing the national anthem.'

Ella took four curtain calls, the Rialto seemed to vibrate to the din of applause, the clapping and cheering, the shouted bravos. Tallying the box office takings in White's office, the theatre-owner and Max traded triumphant grins.

'She's money in the bank, Max.' White enthused. 'The second and third shows are booked out, so this will be the most profitable three-night act here since the Rialto opened for business.'

'Ella's at her peak,' declared Max.

'Listen, friend, a word of advice,' said White. 'The repertoire is your business and hers, mostly hers I guess. But, if you can influence her . . . '

'I try, Gus. What's your advice?'

'Tomorrow and the night after, she should close with that same song. It's popular, Max. The applause was proof enough, right?'

'Seemed to hit 'em where they live. Great idea, Gus. It was her choice. I'll compliment her on it — cunningly — and that should do the trick.'

'You find her hard to handle?'

'Gus — if you knew *how* hard . . . '

When, over breakfast next morning, Max paid Ella the compliment, eagerly supported by Geraldo, she reached as he expected, loftily assuring them that, when it came to 'milking' the ticket-buyers, she was an expert. *Believe Me If All Those Endearing Young Charms* would be retained as her closing number.

The second performance was as big a hit, though the star's mood seemed to worsen with every passing hour. Here in Granger City, it was becoming obvious all employees of the Rialto Theatre and the Kingsley Hotel were wise to her weakness, actually conspiring with her manager and accompanist, and especially with her handsome, ever-alert bodyguard, to deprive her of the cup that cheers. She hated to be beaten. Her enemies were winning the battle.

With Hattie, she was as spiteful as ever, resorting to every insult that came to mind, but 'Inger Schmidt' was consistently unflappable.

With Rick, she was wary, all the time wondering how this urbane character could stay one jump ahead of her, anticipating, reading her mind, ready for anything every moment. Max and Geraldo had known her longer and were wise to her ways. But, when it came to intuition, Rick Braddock seemed to possess more than his share.

No hitches on the third night, just one backstage mishap of which the audience was unaware. Ella was in good voice as usual, the centre of attention. Max and Gus White observing her from the wings left of stage, Rick and Hattie from the right, when a passing stagehand toting a fire bucket tripped. He lurched against Hattie, a short man with the bucket balanced on his shoulder — until that moment.

Sand showered her head. He caught the bucket before it could hit the floor.

'Sorry,' he whispered.

'*Himmel*!' she gasped.

As the stagehand moved on, Rick began flicking sand from her hand and shoulders.

'Thanks, but too late,' she grumbled. 'Why does . . . ?'

'Not so loud, honey,' he cautioned. She dropped her voice to a low murmur.

'Why does sand have to be so *penetrating*? I'm starting to itch already — and it's in my hair. I'll be first in the bathroom tonight.'

'Too bad I can't offer to wash your back.'

'Herr Braddock! Vot a vicked zing to zay!'

'That's something I'll miss when this assignment's finished. Inger's cute kraut accent.'

Ella's admirers listened enraptured to her last song. *Believe Me If All Those Endearing Young Charms* was beginning to bore her, but she sang it as sweetly, as expressively as before, perhaps even more so. There was a ten-second silence, a hush during which the last clear note seemed to hang in the air. Came then the crowd's delayed reaction, an explosion of applause, everybody on their feet to accord her a thunderous standing ovation. Max rubbed his hands in glee. Geraldo did his impulsive gallant bit, overturning the piano stool in his haste to reach her, dropping to one knee before taking her hand and kissing it. How else could Ella respond? She blew kisses and smiled her radiant smile.

'Greatest performance yet!' chortled Max. 'I tell you, Gus, she can still take my breath away!'

'If that gorgeous woman becomes a drunk and has to quit show business,' the theatre-owner said fervently, 'it'll be as lowdown a crime as some madman cutting her throat.'

The troupe would return to the

hotel later this night. There were six curtain calls, after which the eleven-year-old daughter of the mayor of Granger City was ushered on stage by her proud parents to present the star with a floral tribute. Ella accepted it graciously and then, holding the bouquet to her bosom, bent to bestow a kiss on the child.

When he was finally able to win silence, the mayor delivered a five-minute speech, thanking 'the legendary Miss Ella Cardew' and her manager, accompanist and other associates for honouring this community with three outstanding performances destined to be remembered for years to come.

Max responded on his star's behalf with his customary finesse, contriving to say all the right words in exactly two and a half minutes.

The cheering continued while the local lawmen, plus specially recruited aides, escorted the company across the street to the hotel. With her retinue in tow, Ella climbed the stairs. She was followed into her room by Hattie who, in her Inger accent, reported her slight mishap backstage, mumbled an apology that Madam would have to undress by herself just this once and, just for the hell of it, deftly purloined Ella's soap. A womanly impulse born of curiosity. Would *she* give off that same distinctive, lingering scent?

Later, in his room, Rick was treating himself to a nightcap. He had removed his coat, but had not unstrapped his armpit holstered .38. As on every other night of this tour, he intended scouting the whole vicinity of the Kingsley Hotel before calling it a day.

Just as he finished his drink, he heard the commotion in the corridor, Ella's voice raised in anger, Max and Geraldo trying to placate her. He moved out to join them. Bathrobes covered the mens' night clothes; Ella wore a negligee with a towel draped over a shoulder.

'Okay, friends, why the rumpus?' he asked.

'Use your ears, Rick,' sighed Max,

and gestured to the bathroom door.

Rick cocked an ear. His wife was singing while bathing. It wasn't the first time he had heard Hattie raise her voice in song, but this time was different. She was a natural contralto. Right now, she was singing soprano, and the song was more than familiar. *Believe Me If All Those Endearing Young Charms*.

'How dare she go ahead of me!' fumed Ella. '*I* have first claim on the bathroom! Damn the girl! Not only has she locked herself in there, she's *imitating* me . . .'

'Ella, *caro*, no other voice coulda match yours,' pleaded Geraldo.

'. . . and she's using my soap — the thieving bitch!' cried Ella.

'Probably an honest mistake,' soothed Rick. 'Inger has a tortoise shell soap box exactly like yours.'

'Hey, Rick, you sly dog,' grinned Geraldo, dropping his Italian accent. 'How'd *you* know what kind of soap box Inger owns?'

'I must've seen it sometime,' Rick said offhandedly.

'I want her out of there — *now*!' stormed Ella.

'Give the kid a break,' urged Rick. 'While you were charming your audience . . . '

'As only you can, Ella,' interjected Max.

' . . . minor accident backstage,' continued Rick. 'Sand from a fire pail got tipped over Inger. Wouldn't begrudge her time to bathe, wash her hair, would you?'

Hattie was standing in the bathtub, a knotted towel covering her nakedness from her bosom to five inches above her knees, bending slightly and using another towel to dry her hair — and still singing — when the marauders paused in the alley under the half-open bathroom window.

'That's her,' whispered Waldo Noad.

'The song's a dead giveaway,' nodded Horrie Langland. 'And, just like Bart says, there couldn't be a better time.'

'So what're we waiting for?' grinned Noad.

They climbed the firestairs to the gallery and, from then on, circumstances conspired against Hattie, against the four people in the corridor and also against the kidnappers. Because she was drying her ears at this moment, Hattie didn't hear Noad and Langland climb in. Because Ella hadn't yet begun pounding on the bathroom door, Noad and Langland were unaware she and three men were out there in the corridor. And because Hattie trilled the last note of the song in the second before Langland rendered her unconscious with a hard punch to the back of her head, the people outside had no way of knowing she was in danger.

Holding her upright, Langland lifted her out of the tub with the second towel obscuring her face. Noad whisked the folded laundry bag acquired by Wes Trent from under his coat, shook it out and pulled it over unconscious

Hattie's head and shoulders and down to her ankles. He then drew from a pocket the sealed ransom demand addressed M. Shelley and placed it on a stool. Langland draped the filled sack over a brawny shoulder and, trading complacent grins, they made for the window.

'I insist on bathing before retiring,' Ella snapped at her manager. 'Get that stupid girl out of there — this instant!'

'Well, she's not singing any more,' frowned Max. 'I guess she's almost through, Ella, but do you expect me to break the door down and just haul her out? She mightn't be — uh — covered up yet.'

The marauders had descended the firestairs and were headed for the old house when Ella loosed an unladylike curse and began pounding on the door. Rick's scalp crawled. No response from inside. His wife, as he well knew, was a very special woman, but accidents do happen. What if she had slipped when rising from the bathtub — struck her head?

'Stand clear,' he ordered, and charged the door left shoulder first.

The lock surrendered to the impact. The door swung inward and then he, Ella and the other men were hustling into the bathroom, the empty bathroom filled with the cloying scent of Ella's soap. Startled, Geraldo stated the obvious.

'Hey, she's gone.'

'What in blue blazes . . . ?' blinked Ella.

'That's her robe.' Easily recognizing that garment, Rick's nerves jumped. His gaze fell on the envelope and fear gripped him. Fury too. He was remembering other disappearances, the newspaper story. 'Max, it's got your name on it. Read it fast.'

An agitated Max grabbed for the envelope, tore the flap, extracted the note and read it aloud, while Rick noted the trail of soapy water leading to the closed window. He moved across, raised it and thrust head and shoulders out to scan the gallery and the back street; he used his nose as well as his eyes.

Max finished reading. Sweat beaded on his brow.

'This means . . . ' His voice shook. 'It's kidnapping — and they think they've grabbed Ella!'

Ella's face was suddenly devoid of colour.

'Lord Almighty . . . ' she groaned.

'Plain enough,' growled Rick. His mind was in turmoil, but he was struggling to make it work. 'There's a resemblance and whoever grabbed her worked very fast, which explains their mistake.'

'Hell, Rick, I'm hamstrung!' fretted Max. 'I can't *do* anything for Inger, daren't send for the law. Look, if it's gonna take a hundred thousand — okay. I wouldn't let that Austrian kid suffer . . . '

'I'm responsible — it's *my* fault!' Ella was wide-eyed and trembling, plagued by remorse. 'Max, I swear to God — if she's returned alive — I'll never take another drink. No more liquor. I *swear* it. When I think of how I've treated her, belittled her, insulted her, I could die of shame. I mean what I say, Max!'

'I got one thing going for me,' muttered Rick, turning from the window. 'They probably didn't anticipate we'd find out so soon. If they're headed out of town, I could still catch up with 'em'.

'Too risky,' protested Geraldo. 'You don't even know where to *start* looking.'

'Thanks to Ella's choice of soap, I only have to use my nose,' retorted Rick. 'No offence, Ella.'

Geraldo didn't believe he was saying it, but the words came out; his decision was made.

'I'm coming with you, Rick. Mightn't be much help, but I feel like I got to do *something*.'

'Well,' said Rick, as they moved out of the bathroom. 'It's fortunate you're in show business, Gerry, and used to making quick changes.'

'Two minutes,' promised Geraldo, hurrying to his room.

In his own room, Rick donned hat and coat. His armpit-holstered .38 was a comfort, but maybe not enough. The snatch had been handled speedily, efficiently. The routine was typical of the Five Deadly Shadows he had read of, so all right. Five of them. Some extra comfort then. As he strapped on his Colt and thonged the holster down, he grappled with his fears for Hattie's safety. She meant everything to him but, if he gave in to panic, he'd be no help to her. Panic would be disastrous. He needed self-control now, needed to keep his brain and his reflexes working.

When he re-entered the corridor, Max was ushering a weeping Ella into her room and Geraldo waiting for him, minus wig, attired in a rumpled black suit and toting a derby.

'Out the front way,' Rick said briskly

as they started for the stairs. 'Then along the side alley to that back street — the scent of that damn soap'll be just as strong.'

It assailed his nostrils again when they reached the area behind the hotel, that distinctive, unmistakable smell. The hostage had been carried down the firestairs. Glancing along that narrow street, Rick noted the glow of the tip of a cigar by the rear door of the scruffiest house he had seen in years. Was it too much to hope? Maybe not. These kidnappers were noted for their audacity. Could they be *that* audacious, hold their hostage right here in town? Only one way to find out.

Geraldo began a whispered question. 'What do you . . . ?'

'Just walk along with me,' instructed Rick. 'And let's play this cool. We're just taking a stroll.'

Side by side, they ambled. As they drew abreast of the back door guard, Wes Trent, Rick accorded him a cheery nod. They moved on another twenty yards before Rick called a halt.

'Something?' asked Geraldo.

'*Big* something, Gerry,' Rick said softly. 'I haven't caught a whiff of the scent since we passed that old house.'

'You think that's where . . . ?'

'It's a chance I can't pass up. Now we'll retrace our steps. You be ready to ad-lib when I cue you, okay?'

'I'm with you a hundred percent. Scared. But with you.'

Guessing the back door guard had them in view, Rick patted at his pockets as he turned with Geraldo.

'Damn!' he exclaimed. 'Forgot my wallet!' They approached Trent. 'Getting forgetful.'

'That's real dumb,' chided Geraldo. 'Imagine forgetting your wallet.'

As they passed Trent, Rick flashed him an embarrassed grin.

'Me and my memory,' he complained. 'Left my wallet in my room.'

Trent's only reaction was a shrug of indifference. They walked on and turned the corner to enter the side alley, there to pause for a whispered council of war. Listening to Rick's instructions, Geraldo blinked uneasily.

'Can we — really do it?'

'It'll work, but I'll need that distraction, and that's your chore. If they're keeping the rear door guarded, you can bet your butt they're watching the front. Ready?'

'As I'll ever be.'

They turned the rear corner to come in clear view of the back door guard again, Rick making a show of pocketing his wallet. He then thrust a cigar between his teeth and, as they again drew abreast of Trent, paused.

'Me again,' grinned Rick. 'The dumbhead who leaves his wallet behind? Got a match, friend?'

He was never to know whether or not Trent would oblige. Being close enough to do what needed doing, he did it, straight-arming Trent, his fist slamming to the jaw with stunning impact. As Trent sagged, he brought his knee up. Geraldo winced to the sound of the second impact. Rick caught the man, lowered him to the ground, relieved him of his pistol and passed it to the bug-eyed Geraldo, then found his keys.

'Around front now, Gerry. Give me a minute before you start a diversion.'

'How do I . . . ?'

'Improvise, damn it. Improvise.'

Geraldo scuttled away. Rick waited a long moment, then inserted a key. No result. At his third attempt, he used the right key, heard the doorlock turn. Right hand on the butt of his Colt, he turned the knob and began opening the door, hoping against hope the hinges wouldn't squeal. They didn't.

He stepped quietly into a cluttered kitchen. There was dim light, but not in this room. Beyond it was the entrance to the hallway. He could see clear along it to the front door. It was closed and he had no doubt it was also locked. From under a door to his right, from under another to his left, light shafted out. Two men lounged against the front door, smoking, talking quietly.

It was time for Geraldo to create a diversion.

8

Face to Face With Evil

The two men by the front door were Noad and Langland and, when they heard the quavery voice from the other side of the door, they swapped frowns. The voice was raised in song, the song familiar, but the rendition of low quality. Only a musician as expert as Geraldo could manage to sing *every* note off key.

'In a canyon, in a canyon, excavatin' for a mine,

Dwelt a miner, forty-niner, and his daughter Clementine!'

Watching and waiting, Rick saw the leftside door open. A blonde and bulky man appeared, calling to his cronies.

'Waldo — Horrie — what the hell . . . ?'

'Sounds like a deadbeat, drunk as a

skunk,' chuckled Noad. 'We'll get rid of him fast.'

He unlocked and opened the door to appraise a bald man he couldn't recall seeing before. Gerry interrupted his song, held out his derby and begged,

'Just a few dimes in the hat, sir, maybe a whole dollar? I ain't had a square meal in three days.'

'On your way, booze-hound,' ordered Langland.

With Walston watching his cohorts, Rick made his move, drawing his Colt, advancing quietly along the hall. He pressed the weapon's muzzle to the blond man's neck and whispered,

'Point to where you're holding the woman — or you're a dead kidnapper.'

Walston stiffened in shock. Gerry was pleading louder now, engaging the full attention of the other man. Rick prodded harder. Walston gulped and pointed to the door to the right.

'Much obliged,' acknowledged Rick.

He raised his Colt high and brought it down on Walston's head with savage force. Out cold, Walston collapsed, and the resounding thud alerted Noad and Langland. They whirled, right hands snaking to their shoulder-holsters and Rick showed no mercy. Gerry darted clear of the open front doorway as Rick hammered back, fired, recocked and fired again.

Noad was still drawing, Langland's gun out and levelled, when the bullets struck them. The impact drove Noad through the doorway to sprawl lifeless on the porch. Langland's pistol slid from his hand. He pawed at his bloody chest with his face contorted and fell heavily, and then Rick was dashing to the rightside door.

His powerful kick sent the door crashing inward. He followed it into the room, then jerked to a halt.

The scene chilled his blood. On the bed, the laundry sack moved slightly; Hattie was coming to her senses. The nondescript man had risen from his chair at a table on which Rick observed a pad, pen and ink bottle. His teeth were bared, his eyes gleaming — and his cocked .32 levelled at the bundle on the bed.

When he voiced his demand — in such a testy, precise way — Rick realized he was up against a fanatic. If this lean little man were the top brain of the five kidnappers, it was all too clear he was over the edge, caring nought for what must surely follow the din of those two shots, intent only on proving his mastery of the situation.

'Are you so dense as to actually await my command?' he challenged. 'Blind, perhaps? My weapon is pointed at my hostage. You will drop yours — immediately — or Miss Cardew will sing no more. Of course, should you be so foolhardy, you could fire — but no faster than I could shoot this famous lady. *Drop it I say*!'

Rick lowered the hammer on his Colt and tossed it aside. And stalled for time.

'Your hired help seized the wrong party,' he declared. 'Miss Cardew is safe in her hotel room. The only missing member of the group is on that bed. She's Miss Cardew's dresser. And I strongly doubt Max Shelley calculates her to be worth a hundred thousand dollars.'

'You lie — and clumsily.' Renshaw grimaced irritably. 'My men are efficient. I tutored them personally. And I've no patience for fools like you, fools who dare believe they can outwit me.'

'There's always a first time for a mistake, a big one,' retorted Rick. 'Like it or not, you'll have to accept it. That is not Ella Cardew. That's Inger Schmidt.'

'A stupid, desperate lie,' chided Renshaw.

Hattie had revived, and with a raging headache that did not affect her hearing. One of the voices was strange to her; the other as familiar as her own. It didn't take a brilliant mentality to deduce her husband was in a tight fix. Why else would he keep the other man talking? She decided it was time for her voice to be heard, but she was non-Teutonic. The only German phrase she could recall was 'Can anyone here speak German?'

She prefaced the question with a groan of pain.

'*Kann hier jemand Deutsch sprechen?*'

Renshaw tensed. For a moment, his gaze switched from Rick to the bed, and that moment sealed his doom. Too late, he looked Rick's way again. By then, Rick had emptied his armpit holster and was sidestepping. Renshaw loosed a cry of fury and fired. So did Rick and, as Renshaw's bullet missed him, he took no chances, couldn't afford to at such close range, fired again. Mortally wounded, Renshaw lurched like a Saturday night drunk, slumped against the wall coughing blood and, in his last moments, glaring indignantly. His pistol thudded to the floor. He shuddered, sagged to an ungainly squatting posture and died.

Rick dashed to the bed, grasped the top of the sack and wrenched it clear. Hattie lay there, one towel falling away from her throbbing head, the other by some miracle still secure about her body. He bent to kiss her in profound gratitude.

'Dumb question coming up,' he grinned. 'How do you feel?'

'My head aches like crazy and I itch from that damn sack,' she complained. 'Careful, darling! There must be more of them!'

'That pistol popping out front? That'll be Gerry. I guess he's decided the law boys aren't arriving fast enough — as if they aren't already on the way.'

'Help me up. This towel's the only thing between me and an eyeful for my rescuers.'

'You mind if it's Gerry takes you back to the hotel? This place is only a couple of doors away. I'll have to stay, sweetheart. You know how lawmen are. They find three dead men, they *always* ask questions.'

'Can you satisfy them? Do you have all the answers?'

'All of 'em,' Rick declared, raising her from the bed.

Sheriff A. J. Barclay and the deputy working the graveyard patrol had questions aplenty. Just as inquisitive were the locals converging on the house. Carrying his wife to the front porch, Rick addressed the lawmen compellingly. He was at their service, ready with a full explanation, but Miss Inger Schmidt, who had been abducted in mistake for Miss Ella Cardew, needed medical treatment.

Barclay consented to Geraldo's escorting Hattie back to the hotel, then eyed the tall man reholstering his pistols and insisted,

'Whatever you're gonna tell me better make sense.'

'You're gonna be a mighty happy sheriff, especially if you've heard of those kidnappers, the gang the newspapers call the Five Deadly Shadows.'

'This is — *them*?'

'Three dead, two catnapping. They'd better be manacled. Then we'll search them and their baggage while I'm talking. Also, there's something in one of these rooms we should take a look at.'

Cash, so much of it that the lawmens' eyes popped, was found on the three bodies, on the still-befuddled Walston and Trent and in the baggage in the other rooms. Of special significance was the half-completed note on the table near which Renshaw had died. Until the showdown began, the boss-kidnapper had been composing a follow-up to his ransom demand, instructions as to where and how the money was to be delivered.

'This is the clincher, Braddock,' scowled Barclay.

'By the time we're through, you'll have enough evidence to convict the two I clobbered,' nodded Rick. 'Mister Shelley's holding the ransom demand. You could bet your badge the handwriting'll match.'

'And all that cash . . . ' muttered Barclay.

'Collected from kin of their other hostages,' said Rick. 'And I don't need to remind you of the fate of those whose relatives defied them.'

'Lousy, murderin' bastards,' breathed the deputy.

Locals were obeying the lawmens' demands, staying outside. Only one entered the house at first. Estate agent Selwood, roused from sleep by the news of a shooting affray at a property on his books, started convulsively upon recognizing the mortal remains of the boss-kidnapper.

'Special Investigator Ridley of the Pinkerton Agency has been murdered!' he cried.

'Shot in self-defence,' corrected Barclay. 'And, if he was a Pinkerton, I'm your Great-Aunt Lulu Belle. You might as well go back to bed, Mister Selwood. This dump is yours again tomorrow. Meanwhile, we're gonna have to do some more tidying up here.'

After the estate agent had left, Rick

and the sheriff heard the deputy's shouted challenge and moved into the hallway again.

'Hey! Who're you and what d'you think you're doin'?'

A man in dust-streaked range clothes was inspecting the body of the late Horrie Langland, paying particular attention to the hands. Ignoring the deputy's challenge, he advanced along the hall to where Joe Walston lay huddled, hands manacled behind his back, head throbbing. As he hunkered to roll Walston over, Barclay said,

'Better identify yourself, stranger.'

'Name's Noah Gannon — from Deansburg.' Gannon studied the tattoo on the back of the left hand. 'That's a long way from here, Sheriff. So, for me, it's been a long search. But here it ends. See the tattoo? This is one of the two-legged wolves who stole my son and . . . '

'They killed your boy?' frowned Rick.

'Handed him back to me,' said Gannon, rising. 'And that cost me ten thousand.' He offered a terse account of the pay-off, adding that most of the $10,000 had to be borrowed from a Deansburg bank. 'Everything we own, my sister, brother-in-law and me, had to be put up as collateral, the store, the stock, everything. I'd have begged, borrowed or stolen twice that much if they'd demanded it. All I cared about was Toby, getting him back alive. He's only seven years old.'

'Those stinkin' scum,' mumbled the deputy.

'Sheriff, you'll have to contact others who paid ransom,' said Rick. 'Their money should be returned to them.'

'Well, sure,' agreed Barclay. 'But every dollar we've found is evidence. They'll recover what's theirs, but it'll take time.'

'Why should this man have to wait?' pleaded Rick. 'Why not settle up with him here and now? Well, maybe not here and now. Let's say as soon as the banks open tomorrow. He wouldn't want to head all the way back to his home with that much cash in his pockets, risk being ambushed by thieves. A draft forwarded to his bank at Deansburg would be the safe way.'

'Look, Braddock, I'll allow you're a smart detective and I give you credit for nailing a kidnap gang,' said Barclay. 'But I can't hand over ten thousand to a man I never saw before.' He turned to Gannon. 'No offence but, as sheriff, I got certain responsibilities.'

'You can trust him,' said Rick. 'I do.'

'But . . . ' began Barclay.

'Think about it,' urged Rick. 'He's identified one of them. What's more, you can easily verify his claims. All you need do is wire the manager of the bank that granted him the loan. You can also wire the Deansburg law authorities to confirm that he and two relatives own a store there. Mister Gannon doesn't look like a fool to me. I believe everything he's told you can be substantiated.'

'I don't mind waiting, Sheriff,' said

Gannon. 'I'll give you all the names you need — and even stay with you when you send those wires and wait for the replies.'

'You understand that's how it'll have to be done!' challenged Barclay.

'Sure,' nodded Gannon. 'You got your duty.' And now he studied Rick intently 'Braddock's your name? Well, I appreciate your trust.' He offered his hand. 'My given name's Noah.'

'Rickard — called Rick,' responded Rick. During that firm handshake, he sadly remarked, 'I believe we're sharing the same thought, Noah. Your son survived. Other hostages . . . '

'Weren't so lucky,' sighed Gannon. 'I read the newspapers, so I know.'

'I swear, of all the outlaw trash I ever heard of . . . ' Barclay shook his head grimly, 'this bunch, these buzzards, are the lowest, the worst of the worst.' He nodded to his deputy. 'We'll lock up the two soreheads now and have an undertaker come pick up the stiffs. You got all the cash?'

242

'Packed tight in this here valise,' said the deputy.

'Quarter before nine, Gannon, my office,' said Barclay. 'You got someplace to stay?'

'I'll find a place,' said Gannon.

'Sorry you won't get much sleep, Braddock, but you'd better come see me around nine,' insisted Barclay. 'You know the rules. I'll need an affidavit from you and from whoever helped you.'

'His name's Geraldo Palestrina,' offered Rick. 'But don't let that throw you. He speaks English. I can go now? Like to check on Miss Schmidt.'

'See you in the morning,' said Barclay.

'Rick,' said Gannon, as Rick turned to leave.

'Something else?' asked Rick.

'Thanks again,' said Gannon.

'My pleasure,' grinned Rick.

He returned to the hotel in good humour, though in no doubt that memories of his wife's close call would haunt him for a long time to come.

After climbing the stairs, he at once reflected it was fortunate the company would not be resuming the tour on an early morning train. They were scheduled to depart on a south-bound leaving 1 pm. Just as well. Geraldo had changed back to his night attire. He, Ella and Max weren't in their rooms; they were waiting for him in the corridor.

'By golly, Rick . . . ' began Max.

'I told 'em everything, Rick,' said Geraldo. 'Had to. Ella was threatening to strangle me.'

'Everybody has a right to know,' shrugged Rick. 'Now that it's all over, I don't need to hold anything back.' He eyed Ella, a different Ella. She was scrutinizing him anxiously, showing genuine concern. Ella? Genuinely concerned for somebody other than Ella? 'Relax. I said it's all over, and that's for sure.'

'You fought — five bloodthirsty blackguards — who believed they'd kidnapped *me*,' she breathed.

'Five,' shuddered Max.

'Come on now,' Rick cajoled. 'Not the first time I got into a shootout since you hired me. All part of the service, Max. Now how about Inger?'

'I put her to bed — as lovingly as if she were my own sister,' said Ella. 'Sat with her while the doctor examined her. She has a nasty bruise behind one ear, but there's no concussion and she's no longer in pain.' To his amusement, she clutched at his lapels. 'Rick, she *suffered* on my account! I'll never forgive myself for that!'

'Don't distress yourself,' he frowned. 'I'm sure she understands.'

'She's so forgiving,' she murmured. 'I've been a bitch, but she bears me no malice.'

'Ella feels a whole lot different about Inger now,' offered Max. He added gratefully, 'About everything.'

'No more booze,' grinned Geraldo.

'I know you'll hold to your word, honey,' said Max, patting her arm.

'That pledge.' He raised his eyes to the ceiling. 'You made it to Somebody more important than I'll ever be.'

'Best decision you ever made anyway, Ella,' declared Rick. She didn't flinch when he slid an arm about her and gave her a big brotherly hug. 'Better for Max's nerves and better for your beautiful self.'

'I realize that,' she nodded. 'Finally.'

'This whole thing was a bad shock for you,' Max remarked solicitously. 'Maybe a shock you needed.'

'Again I agree, Max,' she said. 'There'll be no more tension, I assure you. No more arguments. From now till this tour ends, we'll be five affectionate friends working together.'

'Max, Gerry, that statement was made by an intelligent lady with a good heart,' grinned Rick. 'And now, if Inger's still awake, I think I should look in on her.'

'I'm coming with you,' said Ella. He raised his eyebrows as she took his arm. 'I insist, Rick dear. She's in bed. She's

246

single and so are you. Showfolk aren't as contemptuous of the proprieties as you might think.'

'You're gonna be chaperone?'

'Better believe it, big boy. Max, Gerry, go to bed. You're dead on your feet.'

Rick moved into his wife's room with Ella in close attendance. The lamp was turned low. Propped up by pillows, Hattie was waiting patiently, and he knew why. No sleep for her till she was assured Sheriff Barclay had accepted her husband's explanation.

Ella perched on the edge of the mattress and took Hattie's hand. Rick drew up a chair and put his first question.

'Feeling better now, Inger?'

'*Ja*,' smiled Hattie. 'Vill sleep *gut. Bitte, Herr* Braddock. *Der Polizei* . . . ?'

'No problems,' soothed Rick. 'Sheriff Barclay's a happy man. The men who kidnapped you — believing they were kidnapping Ella — were part of a five-man gang. Their speciality was seizing hostages, holding them to ransom and, if the ransom wasn't paid, murdering those hostages. Bad people, Inger, the worst kind, so it doesn't bother me that I had to gun down three of them and that the other two will be tried, convicted and executed. That's all you need to know, Inger honey. I did what I had to do and the sheriff heartily agrees.'

'You are *sehr heroisch*,' she enthused.

'And you're a mighty brave lady,' he complimented her.

'That she is,' Ella warmly agreed. 'And you remember what I said, Inger dear. You're still my dresser till we reach Los Angeles, but my friend too.'

'I steal your zoap,' Hattie said contritely.

'Help yourself any time,' chuckled Ella, then waxed curious. 'Rick, is that really how you found your way to her — the scent of my soap?'

'Lady, don't underestimate it,' said Rick.

'It's that strong?' she challenged.

'Don't get me wrong,' he said. 'It's easy on the nose, Ella, a pleasing aroma, but it never quits.' He got to his feet. 'Pleasant dreams, my little apple strudel. See you for breakfast. A late breakfast.'

He left with Ella and walked her to her bedroom.

'Same goes for me,' she remarked. 'Suddenly, I can barely keep my eyes open.'

'Sleep the sleep of the just,' urged Rick. 'Never forget you're travelling with the best kind of friends, people who really care about you.'

'When you first told me you admire me, was that just a line?' she demanded. 'The truth, Rick. If we're really friends now, we shouldn't lie to each other.'

'Meant it that first time,' he assured her. 'Mean it even more now. The change in you, the way you now appreciate Inger for the kind of girl she is — those are the marks of a real lady. And a true star.'

249

She smiled wearily. He opened the door for her and, after she moved inside, closed it and returned to his own room.

★ ★ ★

They sat down to a fine breakfast at 10 am, Ella all smiles, the men relaxed, refreshed by sleep, Hattie her cheery self again.

'Sheriff Barclay won't mind our being late for our appointment with him, Gerry,' Rick said reassuringly.

'Sure he won't be mad at us?' asked Geraldo.

'He'll guess we slept late, and didn't we deserve to?' shrugged Rick.

'He needs statements?' demanded Max.

'It's just routine,' said Rick. 'Don't worry, Max. We'll make the depot with time to spare.'

'I'm going to suggest that we put all memories of last night's ordeal behind us and confine our conversation to a pleasant subject — the tour,' Ella said firmly.

'That's my star,' approved Max. 'Let's talk shop. Listen now, honey, your choice of a song to close the show here was just fine, but . . . '

'Our audiences loved it,' she agreed. 'I have to say, though, it was starting to bore me.'

'Well . . . ' Max eyed her cautiously, 'Gerry had a brainwave. Old song. Still — uh — you're the star, so it has to be your decision.'

'Will you stop being so jittery?' she good-humouredly chided. 'If Gerry has an idea, I want to hear it. You're my manager, he's my accompanist and musical mentor.' She bestowed an encouraging smile on Gerry. 'Let me hear it. I'll listen — if you promise to drop the fake wop accent.'

'It's full of sentiment, Ella baby,' enthused Gerry. 'The crowds'll have to dry their eyes before they gets their butts off their seats and cheer you like crazy. 'Home Sweet Home'. I'll work up a slow and kinda wistful backing, you'll give it that sure-fire Cardew treatment and . . . '

'One of your better ideas, Gerry darling,' she approved. 'I love it. The perfect finale.'

Another milestone. It was clear to the Braddocks, Max and Geraldo that the new, sweet-tempered and co-operative Ella was here to stay, a woman who, though she didn't realize it, might have become an alcoholic within two years, or sooner, but for the emotional shock that had changed her whole outlook. She had made a vow and would hold to it the rest of her life.

The remainder of the tour won welcome publicity, every newspaper along the route to Los Angeles proclaiming Ella as the favourite of frontier folk, as big a success as such luminaries as the great Shakespearian actor, Edwin Booth, and that sprightly legend of vaudeville, Eddie Foy. Travelling by rail or stagecoach, the star was congenial company for her companions, never complaining, always in good humour and high spirits and continuing to enslave the ticket-buyers.

When, at long last, the troupe disembarked at the Los Angeles railroad depot, there were mixed feelings all round. The tour had been a triumph, especially in the financial sense. Upon returning to San Francisco, Ella would continue her career under her manager's guidance and with Geraldo her loyal accompanist. There were regrets, however, that this was a time of parting. Ella's bodyguard and dresser had completed their assignment to the satisfaction of all concerned and, after a final farewell, would stay in Los Angeles to board the next eastbound train and begin their journey home to Denver.

The Braddocks weren't as dejected as the showfolk, but tried not to show it.

'I'll miss you — dear Inger,' Ella declared with deep sincerity, and embraced her.

'*Und* I never forget you,' Hattie assured her.

While she exchanged a few last words with Ella and Geraldo, her husband was drawn to one side by Max. A sealed envelope changed hands.

'Payment in full — plus, Rick old buddy,' muttered Max. 'The agreed fee, plenty to cover extra expenses and — this oughtn't surprise you — a fat bonus. I mean *real* fat. You sure earned it and, because Ella was a smash, I can afford it.'

'Doing business with you has been a pleasure, Max,' Rick responded. 'And quite an experience.'

They rejoined the others, Hattie smiled and nodded as Max handed her the second sealed envelope.

'In cash, Inger honey,' he told her. 'You're a good kid, best dresser Ella ever had. Doesn't she keep saying so? I just hope you'll travel home safe, because that's quite a bundle you're stashing in your purse.'

'Inger'll travel safe, I guarantee,' said

Rick. 'I'll be with her every mile of the way, so she'll be under my protection. In fact . . . ' He surveyed Hattie thoughtfully, 'she quite appeals to me. I may even decide to marry her so as to take better care of her.'

'You — *what*?' Max gaped at him. Ella's eyebrows shot up and Geraldo shook his head dazedly. 'You can say it just like that?'

'Damn it, Rick . . . ' began Geraldo.

Before Ella could speak, Hattie took her cue and played along, beaming at Rick.

'You vish me for your vife, Herr Braddock?'

'You may call me Rick,' he offered grandly.

'*Sehr gut*!' she giggled. 'How zoon ve get married?'

'How about today?' he suggested. 'I'm sure some city official will oblige. A JP. A Lutheran pastor if you prefer.'

'Well, by golly, congratulations!' grinned Max.

'Rick Braddock, if you're determined

to go through with this, you'd better be kind and faithful to my Inger,' Ella warned with her eyes sparkling.

'Too bad we can't stay on for the wedding, but I'm gonna kiss the bride,' chuckled Max.

'Me too,' leered Geraldo.

'I think I'll kiss the bridegroom,' decided Ella, and did so.

Twenty-four hours later, the Braddocks were travelling in style. A tally of the contents of both envelopes assured them the Braddock Detective Agency was well and truly in the black, still operating at a steady profit. Another case closed and now, in the comfort of a private compartment on an eastbound train, they could review recent adventures, recent close calls and involvement in a life style with which they were familiar — the hurly burly of a travelling show.

'A well-paid assignment, darling,' reflected Hattie. 'But we earned every dollar of our fee and all Max's generous extras. Ella's signing the pledge will be worth a fortune to him — and add years to her career and her life.'

'Another success for us,' Rick agreed. 'Nevertheless, your sleep could be disturbed for a while.'

'You anticipate a nightmare or two?' she challenged.

'Those killers stole you away from me for a while,' he said grimly. 'Your life was in the balance, Hattie. It was only for a little while — thanks to the long-lasting scent of Ella's soap — but that was a bad time for both of us. I'm human. I'm the typical devoted husband and, until I pulled that sack off you, I was out of my mind, scared stiff for you.'

'*Never* out of your mind, dear heart,' she countered. 'Your reflexes didn't fail you. Who else but Rick Braddock could suspect such a foxy move, such audacity? The man who planned that abduction *was* audacious, we have to admit that. A hostage hidden such a short distance from where she'd been seized? That was brilliant, you have to admit.'

'Not really,' he argued. 'That crazy-eyed little weasel, the last man I shot, must've thought himself invincible. He overdid it, sweetheart. He'd been audacious before. This time, he was *too* audacious, and it backfired on him.' He grimaced in disgust. 'Lowdown, homicidal little . . . '

'Relax, lover.' Hattie showed him a comforting smile and a sly wink. 'Law-breakers. They're all cunning, but so are the Braddocks. And, when it comes to audacity, we do pretty well ourselves, as if I need to remind you.'

'We have to,' he grinned.

'And we'll continue to be,' she predicted.

'When we get back to Denver,' he grinned, 'remind me to buy you some fine new gowns and take you to dinner and a theatre — best seats in the house.'

'*Sehr gut*!' chuckled Hattie.